Lizzie's Lost Girls
A DIGEST OF UNFOLDING HORROR
BOOK TWO

By

E. R. RUSSELL

For Michelle ♥

Truly There is No Comfort

They turned down a small side street that bordered a pond on one side. Dense trees with branches reached across to each other like dance partners. They shielded the street below from a sun that strained to peek through the leaves. The road was dappled with its rays. A man walked along the shoulder with a rifle in one hand and a string of fish and fishing rod in the other. Hearing a vehicle approaching, he stopped to see who was coming. Lizzie slowed and stopped beside him.

"Howdy," he said as he greeted them with a face that was welcoming and cautious at the same time.

Both Lizzie and Kenya said hello in response. Lizzie looked at the man, tried to gauge what kind of person he might be.

"I think I took a wrong turn," Lizzie said. "We were trying to get around a pile-up. Are we far from route seventeen?"

"Nope. Not far. Seen a lot of those man-eaters today?" the man asked.

"Probably as many as we've seen every day since it all fell apart. Is seventeen far from here?" Lizzie asked again wishing that they had a road atlas.

"So that wreck is still there? Guess there's no one to clean it up. There was a minivan come down here yesterday with a buncha little kids drivin'," he said.

As Lizzie listened for an answer that once again didn't come, she caught on to the last thing he said.

"There were little kids driving a minivan?" Kenya asked excitedly before Lizzie had a chance.

"Yeah! What did they look like?" Lizzie asked excitedly.

"I'll tell you what I told them. Continue down this street until you hit a T-intersection. Take a right and it'll getcha right back to sev'teen."

"Were there five kids? Four girls and a boy?" Lizzie asked slowly and sternly.

"Sounds 'bout right."

"Were they alright?" Lizzie shouted.

"Yeah, they were here. Yesterday, I think it was. I sent them off with some gas that we traded for," the man in the fishing hat said with his shotgun resting on his shoulder.

"Were they okay?" Lizzie asked frantically.

"Only five gallons, just cuz I felt bad for 'em. Anyone else, I would'na even."

"Were they okay?" Lizzie shouted again.

"Okay? Yeah, they were okay," he finally answered.

"How long ago were they here? What did you trade for the gas?"

"Box of shotgun shells."

"They had shotgun shells? Where did they get shotgun shells?" Lizzie asked incredulously, more to herself than to him.

"Yes ma'am, sure did. They had several, in fact. They offered me money and Gatorade but I couldn't take that from them. I got plenty to eat and drink. Been plannin' on this for years."

"Years? For years you've been planning on people seemingly coming back to life after dying and then eating the living?" Lizzie asked more sarcastically than with any level of seriousness.

"Gotta say, this was a surprise. I was expectin' a Al Qaeda terrorist strike takin' out our guv'ment or some kind of biowarfare bug in the water. You know, somethin' like that. I didn't expect anything like this."

Kenya peered across from the passenger seat looking at the man standing there with his dirty yellow fishing hat with one lure on it, an unlit cigarette with a bent tip dangling from the corner of his mouth that bobbed when he spoke. An older man, with long, graying hair hanging from beneath the hat, he wore a stained polo shirt and plaid Bermuda shorts.

"When I was a kid, they brought Ebola into our neighborhood. There was this guv'ment buildin' all secret-like with its comins and goins. Seems they brought a buncha monkeys from some godforsaken country in there and was doin' all these tests. We didn't know until years later just how close we came to total 'nialation."

"So, wait," Lizzie paused and took off her sunglasses. "Are you saying that you're one of those crazy doomsday preppers?"

"I wouldn't exactly call it crazy, now. Would you?" He answered dropping the rifle to his side. "I might not be one of those 'crazy doomsday preppers' as you put it, but I had some things ready just in case," he paused and took a lazy look around. "But like I said, I thought somethin' would happen eventually."

Lizzie looked at him, looked through the windshield at the foliaged road laid out in front of them and nodded her head.

"Ya know, you're right. All these years, in the back of my head, I thought the same thing. 9/11, anthrax, terrorists, mass shootings, North Korea, wasn't any of those, now was it? Looks like we were right in thinking *something* would happen," Lizzie looked up at the man, her eyes squinting in response to the bright sky. "I just wasn't planning for it like you were. I thought about it once in a while, bought a few more canned goods than I needed when they were on sale, but basically did nothing. So how long ago did you say it was that you traded with them?"

"Yesterday 'round noon, it was," he finally answered.

The man shifted his feet and took a step back from the car. He looked down the street in front of them and then behind them.

"Well, good luck to you," he said and put his rifle back on this shoulder.

"Same to you," Lizzie replied and slowly drove off slapping Kenya on the thigh and screamed with a jubilant smile on her face. "They have to be at my parents by now, Kenya! They have to be there by now!"

They came to the T-intersection, took the right and Lizzie floored it.

They pulled into the driveway of the modest home on Cricket Lane, the house that Lizzie grew up in. The shades were drawn, the front door closed. It looked desolate, deserted. Slowly, Lizzie and Kenya got out of the car and surveyed the house before them. Lizzie reached into the big pocket on the front of her barn coat and grabbed her keychain. The ring tended to weigh her coat down from the number of keys she had.

Just as Lizzie slid her parent's housekey into the lock of the door, the door opened. It pulled the jumble of keys out of her hand because the keys were still engaged in the lock. They swung and tinkled. A tall man with graying hair and a soft, kind face stood and looked at her blankly.

"Mr. Harvey?" Lizzie asked incredulously and the man's face broke into a wide beaming smile. "Are my parents here?"

"They sure are! We're just hunkered down in here. Come on in, Lizzie." He said as he stepped back and broadened the entrance to admit them.

Lizzie and Kenya stepped through the threshold and into the small foyer. Lizzie walked into the parlor and wondered where her parents were. The house was eerily quiet. Kenya came in behind her. As Lizzie took off her big barn coat and draped it over a chair, they could hear the mechanism of the dead bolt as it secured the front door locking them in.

"It sure is good to see a familiar face. I haven't seen you in a dog's age. Who's this you've got with you?" He asked as he joined them in the parlor.

"This is Kenya. I'm looking for my kids. Are they here?"

"No, honey, they aren't. It's just your parents and me," Mr. Harvey responded. "Your father is out tinkering with something in the shed and your mom is down in the basement looking for something. Why don't you go down and surprise her?"

"Sure," Lizzie frowned thinking that the kids should have already been at the house. She went toward the back of the house to the kitchen to go down to the basement.

"Kenya, why don't you have a seat and take a load off?" Mr. Harvey said over his shoulder as he followed Lizzie to the kitchen.

Lizzie opened the basement door calling out to her mother only to be met by silence. She went down a couple of steps and called out to her mother again and heard nothing. What she did hear was the door being slammed shut behind her and the lock being slid across the metal slide on the kitchen side of the door. She ran back up the stairs, hammering on the door with her fists and screaming for Mr. Harvey to open it with no response from the other side.

Lizzie heard Mr. Harvey's footsteps leaving the kitchen and heading to the front of the house. The next sound she heard was Kenya screaming and yelling, "No! Get off me!"

Lizzie could hear two bodies bumping around, banging against walls and furniture. She could hear Kenya being hit and crying and fighting.

Lizzie put her ear up against the door to listen and to think. Kenya was screaming for Lizzie to help her and just screaming in general. Lizzie resumed banging on the door while trying to find some leverage. She wanted to throw her body against the door to force it open and then something occurred to her.

Soon after her parents moved into this house they put on an addition when they found out that they were expecting a new little baby to join a family that was thought to already have been complete. Sadly, the new baby never arrived but they still had the new addition with a full basement.

Prior to construction, there had been the original root cellar that would be more aptly called a crawl space since it was only about four feet deep. It was under the original part of the house. It had only been accessible from a bulkhead in the backyard. The new full basement added with the new construction and the old root cellar were connected by a small door that would give Lizzie access to the bulkhead and thus, to the backyard.

Lizzie ran down the stairs and over to the little door that was set up off the floor about two feet and opened it. It was too dark to see in and she couldn't remember where the pull string for the light was. She grabbed a flashlight off a shelf and climbed into the cobwebbed hollow void.

Walking crouched over with cobwebs catching on her hair, her feet scuffed along the dirt floor. Reaching the wooden bulkhead doors, she unhooked the unlocked padlock and slowly pushed open one of the doors. Lizzie kept careful hold of the door so that it wouldn't fall open crashing against the frame and alerting Mr. Harvey of her whereabouts.

Up the five or so wooden plank stairs and hugging the walls of the house, Lizzie made her way around to the front careful to duck low below the windows. Even from outside of the house she could hear Kenya screaming, crying and pleading.

She ran quickly to the car, opened the driver's side door and pulled the lever to open the trunk. Lizzie crawled around to the truck and sifted through the contents looking for one or both of Dan's rifle cases. Instead, she found a small, soft-sided gun case. She unzipped the case to find a second Glock 40. Dan hadn't said that he had two, but he had said that he'd been out shooting recently. Carefully pulling out the gun, she popped the clip and checked that it was full. Kenya's screaming kicked up a crescendo and that spurred Lizzie to getting to the door without care.

Her keys still hung in the lock which surprised and elated her. She quietly turned the deadbolt lock. The next obstacle was opening the front door without its customary squeak. She was grateful for the keys being in the lock but concerned about what the squeaking door might bring. She slowly pushed open the door and there it was, the squeaky hinge.

"Who's out there?" Mr. Harvey bellowed and met Lizzie in the parlor. "How the fuck did you get out, you bitch?"

Lizzie didn't expect him to be in the parlor so quickly and his sudden appearance startled her. She took a shot at him, but the surprise and her haste caused her to miss. She decided to run at full speed into him to knock him down. At the same time, he lunged at her swinging as he came, and the punch landed hard on her cheek bone below her eye. Her right eye exploded into fireworks that were not celebrating the birth of the United States. The force of the hit caused Lizzie to fall to the floor landing hard on her tailbone and she saw stars.

Mr. Harvey kicked her head, screaming obscenities and telling her that she was going to get what her mother had gotten and then some, but she would just have to wait her turn. He looked at her for a second, shaking his head and thinking. Mr. Harvey drew back his leg and kicked her in the stomach. He left her lying on the floor immobilized in pain, curled into a ball. He went back toward the kitchen, his steps heavy, slow and deliberate. "Now, just what the fuck do you think you're doing?" Lizzie heard him say.

The pain in Lizzie's head was strikingly intense like a knife being jabbed into a Halloween pumpkin. She hoped her head would detonate like some bomb releasing shards of pain in the form of bb's and screws relieving her from the fiery ache that had her nerve endings dancing on a bed of nails. She'd had her share of headaches, but this was something beyond the full blown bangaroos she was used to once a month. She didn't want to ever move again, instead opting to just curl up as tightly as possible into a ball, give in and give up.

Just as she was surrendering, a piercing, primal scream issuing forth from the depth of Kenya's soul pulled Lizzie out of the haze of the pounding, throbbing hell trapping her in her body and reminded her of what she needed to do. She opened her eyes but really only the left one opened, the right was just a slit at this point.

She scanned the floor, the room for the Glock but didn't see it. What she did see were the fireplace tools with a poker standing among them.

Lizzie painstakingly pulled herself to her hands and knees with silenced groans stuffed deep into her belly. Her face winced with every movement. Crawling to the fireplace through the dizziness and explosions timed to her heartbeat exploding in her head, it was like Mr. Harvey was kicking her over and over again.

When she got to the fireplace, she reached up grabbing the mantle to pull herself to her feet. As she rose, she saw the family photos her mother had so lovingly taken, framed and placed, each of which marked moments, achievements and happier times that depicted the narrative of this family's life. Lizzie's favorite was always her parent's wedding picture. She could and had stared at it for hours over the course of her life. Her mother had always been picking it up off the sofa or coffee table to place it back on the mantle after she and/or her sister had a gazing session with it and usually a story-telling hour having created their own fairy tale version of the day.

The wedding had taken place in 1971, three months after Lizzie's father had returned from Vietnam. He stood next to her mother in a simple white tuxedo jacket and black tuxedo pants with an unemotional face contrasted with his bride's beaming ear to ear smile.

As a little girl, she mostly just stared at her mother's wedding dress pouring over every detail. The dress was high necked, high wasted with long sleeves gathered at the wrist. The bodice and skirt had a simple lace that overlay the satin. The skirt was straight and aside from the lace overlay there was no embellishment. Beneath a large billowing veil, her mother's hair hung to her shoulders with the ends flipped up. All Lizzie wanted was to grow up and wear her mother's dress at her own wedding and have her own fairy tale day.

It wasn't until she was older when Lizzie finally noticed that her dad's smile didn't match her mother's. She only ever thought of her dad as a happy, smiling, jovial guy. Whenever she asked him why he wasn't smiling in the wedding pictures, he would say that the photographer had caught him at the wrong moment because his wedding day was one of the three happiest days of his life, the other two were when she and her sister were born.

Growing older and becoming more acquainted with the world, Lizzie wasn't as placated as she once was with her father's response. She asked her mother about it. Her mother told her that he looked like that for a long time. She blamed Vietnam and said that he'd been through a lot during the war. He'd once mentioned something that had happened in Cambodia but would not give details. Most of what she knew was gathered from his nightmares and the very occasional remark. She knew he would need time to recover from all he'd seen and done while in-country.

Lizzie's mother had told her that one day as she was knee-deep in her flower garden pulling weeds, she looked up at him. He was edging the sidewalk and there was a smile on his face. She looked at him several times and each time he had a small, peaceful smile on his face. It was truly there as it had never been before, like it went all the way to his insides, deep into his heart. It was genuine and not something he put on his face to pacify the public. It was only there for himself. She never knew what happened to change his demeanor; he never said, and she never asked. Just one day, his scowl left, and it never came back.

At first, Lizzie mistakenly grabbed the broom. She dropped it quickly back into the holder and made sure that she pulled out the poker. She jammed her good eye closed and rubbed it with her balled up fist and felt a momentary lapse of pain. She opened her eye and the pain was back.

Moving haltingly toward the kitchen, each step was hard won. What she saw when she got there incensed and terrified her in alternating and simultaneous waves. Kenya was lying on her stomach with her arms stretched above her head, cuffed to the kitchen bar stool that was mounted to the floor. Mr. Harvey was behind her on his knees between her spread legs. Kenya was trying to kick him and turn her body over, but he had one hand on her back pushing her to the floor and his other hand was doing something else that she couldn't see. As Kenya squirmed and tried to get free, Lizzie could see that the back of her pants had been cut apart revealing Kenya's skin.

Seeing Kenya's bare skin was the impetus she needed. Lizzie stepped into the kitchen winding her arms back holding the poker like a bat. As she swung, Mr. Harvey saw that she was there and started to stand up. Lizzie's goal was to plant the hook of the poker in Mr. Harvey's eye. He saw her approach and turned to face her. He let out a deep grunt when the poker made contact with his neck and he lost his balance.

In an effort to right himself, he grabbed the poker yanking Lizzie toward him. He threw the poker away from them and it hit the kitchen wall. She fell to the floor on her knees and Mr. Harvey fell upon her, punched her again. His fist slid off her cheek rather than landing the impact of a full-force blow. Nonetheless, the subsequent blows hit their targets, lips, nose, cheeks, temple.

As the three bodies writhed on the floor, tangled together, Kenya was able to flip herself over despite her arms being twisted above her head. Even further, she managed to land a few solid kicks onto Mr. Harvey's back. He was impervious to the kicks; instead he had his hands wrapped around Lizzie's neck and was focused on choking her.

Kenya's screaming faded in Lizzie's ears as she was close to blacking out. Lizzie was fighting internally, still determined and desperate to stay in the present. If she let go, if she gave in to the darkness it would be tantamount to not only giving up on Kenya but giving up on her children. Her children would finally arrive here to find her dead and to be welcomed in by this deranged and deadly formerly benign neighbor.

His face was inches from Lizzie's. From his lips emanated vile words falling onto her face via the spittle carrying them. She closed her eyes and then she saw it. There was a segment on a news program demonstrating self-defense techniques that had given instructions on this very situation.

Lizzie drew up all her strength for one last ditch effort. She rocked to the left to create momentum and as she rocked back right she threaded her left arm under his, clasping her hands together as she raised her arms with everything she had left to fight with, again relying on the leftward movement of her rocking body. She broke the hold of his hands on her neck. The force of the unexpected action threw his body off hers and into Kenya's relentlessly pummeling legs. Mr. Harvey fended off Kenya's kicks. He tried to grab one or both of her legs to immobilize her, but it wasn't working. Lizzie jumped to her feet and got to the kitchen island where the Glock sat. She picked up the gun, cocked it and quickly aimed at Mr. Harvey. His back was turned to her as he dealt with Kenya. She shot at the biggest target, his back, and fired. She hit him just below the shoulder blade; he screamed, fell over, lay still and moaned softly.

"Kenya! Kenya! Are you okay?" Lizzie shouted as she scrambled to Kenya's side. Kenya's arms were still twisted around the bar stool pole. She looked at Lizzie and burst out sobbing. Lizzie wiped the tears away with her hands and cooed to her soothingly trying to comfort her. "Do you know if he had a handcuff key?" Kenya shook her head in the negative unable to even utter the word no.

Lizzie crawled over to Mr. Harvey. He was on his stomach with his head turned to the side. Drool was running from his mouth, down his chin and pooling on the floor. She shoved her hands into the back pockets of his pants looking for the key and found nothing. She grunted as she strained to turn him over. He groaned when his back made contact with the floor. His head rolled and then rested. He was quiet and unmoving again.

Reaching into both of his front pants pockets, Lizzie found nothing. She sat back on her haunches and rubbed Kenya's arm. "Give me a second. I'll think of something," She looked at him disgustedly and then saw a string around his neck. Pulling on it revealed a small key. Lizzie yanked it roughly over his head and scrambled over to Kenya to unlock her hands.

Once Kenya was free, she clung to Lizzie and wept inconsolably despite any effort by Lizzie to comfort her. Truly, there is no comfort for an offense of this magnitude.

Their faces close together, Lizzie rocked Kenya. She did what she did as a mother would when one of her babies were hurt. They both heard a groan and then saw Mr. Harvey's foot twitch. Whether he was alive or the new kind of being alive, he was going to have to be dealt with.

"Sweetie, I gotta take care of that," Lizzie said softly. "Think you can make it down to the parlor?" Lizzie said standing up and pulling Kenya with her as she did.

Lizzie watched Kenya slowly make her way down the hall and was reminded that the back of her pants had been cut open, slit down from the waist.

"Sweetie," she said as she scooted after her, "Go on upstairs to my parent's room and find some pants, sweatpants, something that you can put on. When I'm done with him, I'll get your stuff from the car."

By this point, Lizzie had an arm around Kenya and put her hand softly on her face. Lizzie kissed Kenya's cheek and pointed up the staircase.

"First room on the left, okay?"

Kenya took the first two steps, grabbed the banister to steady herself and began to cry anew. She bowed her head and said, "Thanks so much. I'm so sorry."

"Hey, hey, hey! What do you mean?" Lizzie said running around the banister and up a step to hold Kenya. "None of this is your fault. If anything, it's mine. I'm the one who is sorry," she said and squeezed Kenya tight and said, "Now, I'm gonna go take care of that barbaricfuckpig. Okay?" Kenya nodded. "None of this is even remotely your fault. Do you understand me?"

Kenya nodded again and Lizzie went back to the kitchen.

When Lizzie returned, Mr. Harvey was unmoved, lying still on the floor. He was moaning lowly and muttering a bit. Lizzie stood over him thinking about how she wanted to finish him and how she should finish him. In the end, she went with how she should since it would take less time and make less mess.

Once she got the kitchen door propped open, she picked him up with her hands placed under his shoulders and she dragged him out of the kitchen onto the backyard deck. He was no small man. She strained under his weight as she went. She pulled him over to the staircase, walked down a few steps leaving him so that the top part of his body was angled downward toward the bottom of the stairs. She plucked her way back to the top trying not to trip over his body and tumble down the stairs herself. When Lizzie reached the top again, she lifted up his legs throwing them over his head so that his body rolled and fell down step by step until he got caught about two thirds of the way down. She went down a few steps, steadied herself and kicked him back into motion. He landed at the bottom with a loud groan. Lizzie smiled.

Slowly, Lizzie walked down the remaining few stairs one at a time. She took her time. She kicked each foot out in front of her as she went as if to accentuate her movement. He was making noises that sounded like crying but he didn't look like he was crying. He was having problems breathing; more like sucking air in instead of inhaling it.

Reaching the bottom, she stood at his head, squatted, grabbed his arms and pulled him to the side of the backyard where the woods began. It was a slow-going business. His weight wasn't dead yet, but it sure was heavy. Once she had him where she wanted him, she dropped his arms and went back to the house to grab a knife.

Upon her return, she knelt down beside him and he looked at her. He was trying to speak, and it looked he was saying that he was sorry over and over again. Lizzie looked at him with extreme disgust and disdain, pushed his head to the side exposing the temple and pushed the knife in with a strong, deliberate force using both hands, leaning into it with her whole body and twisting the blade a little.

When Lizzie came back into the kitchen, Kenya had changed into sweatpants and was mopping up the blood from the floor with a towel. Her face was stoic, sad and reflective but she was not crying. Lizzie placed Kenya's backpack on the kitchen island and threw the bloody knife into the sink.

Walking slowly over to Kenya, Lizzie dropped to her knees and grabbed a towel, poured some ammonia and started wiping up the blood trail to the door.

"Lizzie, I got this." Kenya said without looking up.

"You shouldn't have t-,"

"I need to do this." Kenya said sternly interrupting Lizzie.

Lizzie stood, scratched Kenya's head through the knit cap affectionately, "I'll get a trash bag."

When the sun rose the next morning, Lizzie was up with it. Kenya wouldn't sleep in one of the other rooms alone so, they slept together in Lizzie's parent's king-sized bed. She left Kenya sleeping and went looking for her parents. With everything that had happened yesterday, Lizzie did not want Kenya with her when or if she found her parents.

Her father had been easy to find. He was in the shed where the garden tools and mowers were. He'd been hit over the head and then knifed at the base of the skull and he lay in the fetal position on the dirt floor near his workbench. The bugs had gotten to him. Looking at insects crawling in and out of the orifices of her father's face and flies lighting on the congealed blood made the canned peaches in Lizzie's stomach churn and she thought she might vomit and there would go breakfast.

Lizzie pulled her dad's two mowers out of the shed, grabbed a tarp, rolled his body onto it and wrapped him in it. She tied bungee cords around him in hopes that a tarp and bungee cords would deter animals from getting to him. In all her life, she never thought so little would be made of her father's death. He was a good man and deserved to have his life honored and celebrated. He did not deserve to be wrapped up in plastic and bungee corded like he never meant anything, never made a contribution to the world.

Given that Mr. Harvey had hinted about what he'd done to her mother, she expected the worst, but what she found was much worse than she could have imagined. Her mother lay face down in vomit on the laundry room floor in the new part of the basement.

This room had been her mother's organizational pride and joy. Combination laundry and sewing room, this was where Lizzie's mother escaped, worked, meditated and at times, recommitted to her marriage in the silence, solace and sanctity of the four yellow walls. This room was her room. This room was where Lizzie found her mother. Face down, the back of her head caved in and her nose looked like it was bent at an unnatural angle. The back of her shirt ripped open revealing blood, bruises and scratch marks. Her pants cut down the back like Kenya's had been and the evidence of violation visible for anyone to see. Visible for anyone to see.

They had nearly made it home in Dan's car yesterday, running out of gas at the top of Cricket Lane. Since Lizzie's parent's cars were conspicuously missing, they had no other choice but to look for gas while they were out looking for the Buckner kids. Kenya carried a red plastic gas jug with a section of cut off garden hose hanging around her neck. It was one survival tip that Lizzie had learned from her dad that she could teach Kenya.

It was still early morning. Lizzie and Kenya walked with conscious purpose and alertness. The air was cool beneath an overcast sky above. It had stopped raining about an hour ago. Who knew if it would start back up? There were no weather forecasters to make their professional guesses and if there were, there was no way to broadcast it.

Kenya was quiet and responded to Lizzie with a yes, no or I don't know. Kenya hadn't spoken much since her experience with Mr. Harvey and that was understandable. There wasn't anything Lizzie could do to change what happened. She just wanted to comfort and support Kenya.

Both of them were bruised and sore. They had matching black eyes and Lizzie had a fat, swollen lip. Lizzie wasn't walking as fast and easy as she would like to be, but she was just happy to be walking.

The air was heavy with the putrid smell of death and smoke and for the first day in a while, it was surprisingly quiet. There was one bird singing in a tree somewhere along the side of the road they walked.

After finding out from the fisherman doomsday prepper that he had seen her kids, Lizzie had every hope she would find them and believed that they couldn't be too far away. They'd been out looking for Lizzie's children in the two days since encountering Mr. Harvey and hadn't picked up so much as a crumb on them.

During their search, they had put down about fifteen dead heads between them. As for living people, they had only seen evidence of life but hadn't seen any on the hoof.

"While we're out, do you know of a library or bookstore we can hit up?" Kenya posed to Lizzie.

"Sure. What are you looking for? My mom has, rather had, a good novel collection at her house," Lizzie responded.

"I'm looking for a survival guide of some sort. I found an old road atlas which will be useful except for new roads or demolished roads but, I was thinking that some kind of survival guide with tips on how to do stuff would be maybe, like, a key to survival without Google and YouTube," Kenya said with an open, raised face.

Lizzie knit her brow and looked at Kenya with a mock seriousness and said, "Good thinking," with a sharp nod of her head.

The Hartwood Town Library was not an exhaustive collection of literature, classical, modern or otherwise on a now defunct civilization. No, the Hartwood Town Library serviced a small rural community with small rural resources and interests.

The library was housed in an old Victorian mansion in what passed as the bustling downtown area. The outer glass double doors that had been added in the 1970's when the mansion had become the town library had been left unlocked. They entered the vestibule which had been the original front porch and faced the original doors made of mahogany with Tiffany stained glass set within them. There was a large patinaed bronze "W" on the lower part of each of the doors. The house had been built by the Whites in 1875, a prominent merchant family.

"This was always the most beautiful building in town that everyone had access to," Lizzie said as she tried the doorknobs on the double Victorian doors and found them locked. She stood back to look at the doors. "The last thing I want to do is try to break in. Let's go around to the back doors and see if any are open."

"This place is humungous," Kenya said in awe as she looked up taking in the height of the building while they walked around it.

The building was three stories with octagonal towers at each side in the front, multiple gables creating an elaborate roof with accentuating dentil work.

"I've never been in a house like this," she added as she followed Lizzie to the back door.

"Well, hold onto your boots. Wait 'til you see the inside of this place," Lizzie said as she climbed the steps to the back door. She tried the handle and again it was locked. "Well, this is unfortunate," she frowned, stood thinking for a second and then said, "Screw it! Stand back a bit."

Lizzie raised the heavy Maglite flashlight she'd been carrying and banged the brass doorknob repeatedly until it hung from its housing. Lizzie twisted and jiggled the knob and managed to get the door open.

"I can't believe that there wasn't a deadbolt, too."

"In this town? I'm surprised the doors were even locked at all," Lizzie answered.

They walked through the doorway and into the kitchen area that had been left in disarray. Despite some light filtering through from between the window frames and blinds, it wasn't bright enough to see the surroundings very well. Lizzie pressed on her Maglite to illuminate their path as their shoes made crunching noises on sugar packets, cereal and the other items scattered across the kitchen's floor. "Where's your flashlight, sweetie? Can you pull it out?"

Kenya slipped one shoulder out of her backpack and her hand roamed around to find the flashlight. "It's right here," she said as she pulled it out and clicked it on. "Where do you think I could find survival books?"

"Well, I wouldn't be surprised if this place still had a card catalog. But if you want to check out the second floor, I'll look down here. I want to get some maps."

"A card what?" Kenya asked with a puzzled face. "I have no idea what you just said."

"Not surprising. Never mind; it was before your time, I guess," Lizzie sighed. "Anyway, it doesn't matter anymore."

They came into the double parlor at the front of the house where the librarian had set up her check out desk. Off to the side, was the large opening to the former ballroom that ran the length of the side of the house. It was now a bookcase lined room with large tables, high backed chairs and small desk lamps down the center. They swept their flashlights over the furniture and walls, looked and listened for boogey men.

"I'm gonna head up to the second floor," Kenya said making her way to the wide staircase near the set of front doors. The floors creaked as she climbed the steps and disappeared into the shadows.

"Be careful and scream if you need me!" Lizzie yelled after her.

Lizzie continued into the front most parlor room marked "Periodicals" and "Reference" and swept her flashlight over the books and racks. She wandered around the reference materials poking through things looking for town and state maps that could be of use to her. Luckily, she managed to yank out of a stack of books a recent edition of a United States atlas. It had been published just a year before which was at least ten years newer than the edition that Kenya had found in a garage.

Creaking came from the ceiling above her head followed by a few heavy, scrambling footsteps and then a heavy thump. Alarmed at once, Lizzie began screaming Kenya's name, calling out for an answer while she ran to the wide, elaborately carved mahogany staircase taking two painful steps at a time.

Lizzie rounded the corner to see Kenya struggling with what had once been a man. He was dressed in khaki colored work clothes. Now, this man was just a dead head ghoul looking for human flavored sushi. The dead head towered over Kenya. She had one hand planted on his face pushing his head as far back as she could to keep its gnashing, chomping mouth from connecting with any part of her.

On the floor a few feet away, lay a crumpled body with Kenya's knife sticking out of its eye. Kenya looked once or twice over at the knife, but it was well out of her reach. Kenya was vehemently fighting off the dead head's grabby hands with her other hand, thwarting its attempts of coming in for a toothy French kiss and more.

Lizzie ran at the former man thing and began swinging her heavy Maglite at his head, slamming the weight of the metal canister into its dome with all her might. She hammered its skull until it finally caved in. The animation left the monster's body and it slid down against Kenya like a deflated balloon. Kenya recoiled sharply, jumping away from it.

"Are you okay, honey? Did he get you anywhere?" Lizzie asked reaching out to pull the girl into a reassuring hug.

"I'm okay," Kenya replied, her face cradled into Lizzie's shoulder. "I saw her coming," she said nodding toward the woman on the floor, "but he came out of nowhere."

"Ah, yes," Lizzie looked at the body on the floor in its neat twinset and skirt, covered in blood, "that was Mrs. Johnston. She loved all the books in this building but couldn't stand us kids being in here using them," Lizzie said as she walked over to the body. She put a foot on Mrs. Johnston's neck, bent over and pulled Kenya's knife out. It made a sucking sound as the flesh let go of the blade. "He must have been the custodian here, not that it matters anymore."

"Tru dat," Kenya responded.

"Did you find what you were looking for?"

"Nope, didn't have a chance."

Walking down Main Street, Kenya leafed through one of the survival guides she had liberated from the Hartwood Public Library after the Librarian and Custodian attack. The book was called, <u>US ARMY SURVIVAL MANUAL</u>. "There are some really cool things we can do in here," Kenya said ruminating over the pages. "There's a ton of stuff on getting water."

"That could come in handy. We'll have to make sure we hang on to these books. Gotta hand it to you kid; it never occurred to me to look for something like that. You're one smart cookie," Lizzie said smiling at Kenya. "I'd like to take a look through those books, too."

They continued looking for Lizzie's children southwest of Lizzie's parent's house. Being on foot, Lizzie felt vulnerable, so she kept one eye to hiding spots and escape routes. Things were already starting to look overgrown with no one no longer attending to their lawns and gardens. There would be no best garden or landscaping awards bestowed this year or likely for some time to come. Debris consisting of formerly useful things littered the streets, fields, parking lots and any place that never would have normally hosted such items. Always the smell of death hung in the air.

As the afternoon's daylight ticked away, Kenya suggested that it might be time to turn back toward home and settle in for the night. They turned onto Washington Street which, of course, was replete with the new apocalyptic décor of discarded items. However, there was something different here. Faint groans and moans could be heard along with the smell of something cooking on a fire and smoke that could be seen rising over the top of an overgrown hedge with branches reaching out for mother sun at random angles.

They came up as slowly and cautiously as they possibly could, attempting to maintain some cover to shield their arrival from whomever was on the other side of the hedge for as long as they could. As they peeked through the holes the branches created, they saw something completely unexpected. Off to the side of the yard, the women saw a gaggle of dead heads of various sizes, shapes and sex. They moved closer to get a better look and they could see that what had once been a flower garden was now a fire pit on the lawn of a stately colonial style home. On one side of the fire was an ornate iron bench and on the other was a man sitting on a small cooler tending to a blob of something being cooked over the fire on a spit.

He stood up and yelled out, "Who's there? I can see you behind the hedges. Why doncha c'mon out?" He had a light brown beard nearly reaching his chest and a bushy mustache covering his mouth. Although some color peaked out between the grime, his clothes were so dirty that they could probably stand in a corner on their own. His short, unkempt hair supported a grease stained, once white trucker cap. His eyes peered out from the filth that nearly closed them in. "C'mon over here." He beckoned to them and waved them over. "I won't bite cha," he stopped, thought a few seconds and continued, "Yeah, I didn't say that to be funny."

Lizzie turned and looked at Kenya and quietly asked, "Where's your gun? Is it ready?"

"Yeah, it's in my waistband."

"Good. Leave it there unless you need it. I have mine in my jacket pocket. I hope we don't need them," Lizzie told her and started walking to the break in the hedges where the sidewalk met the street. Kenya followed akimbo behind her.

"Howdy!" He said as they approached him, and they responded in kind. "C'mon over. Have a seat," he said revealing some teeth but not too many. "Muh name's Chuck. This duck's 'most done. You're welcome to some."

Lizzie and Kenya took a seat on the iron bench across from him with the fire in between, thanking him for his kindness. Neither of them relaxed; they were ready to spring in response to a flinch out of place. They looked at what turned out to be eleven dead heads standing behind Chuck. Each dead head's torso was wrapped in rope so that its arms were pinned down at its sides.

"Um…why do you have them like that?" Kenya warily asked pointing to the group of bobbing bodies. "Who are they?"

"Them?" He said pointing over his shoulder with his thumb not even looking back, "That's muh family. Muh wife's the one in the pokey dots. Them two over yonder are her folks. That guy on the other end is muh daddy and the rest is our keeds, age six to fifteen, yes ma'am."

"What happened? Why do you have them all tied up like that?" Lizzie asked.

"Well, I got home and from what Tommy said, that's muh ten-year-old, muh wife ripped through her folks, Janey and Bobby and then they ripped through the rest. Tommy's the little 'un over by that tree there. He was the last to go," he pointed to a little boy in ripped up, blood covered jeans with a surprisingly serene face and eyes that just stared out at nothing in particular.

"But why do you have them like that?" Kenya pushed for an answer, crinkling her nose.

There was a long pause before he responded. "I heard there's a refugee center in Fredericksburg. Maybe they gut a cure there for this. Maybe they could fix 'em there. They ain't dead, right? Cuz could they be standing there like that if they was? So maybe, they gut somethin' for this sickness there."

"Yeah, maybe they do," Lizzie said trying to offer him a small reassuring smile.

"Say, y'all look kinda beat up like y'all been wrasslin' with a bear. Y'all'kay?" He asked noting both Lizzie and Kenya's bruised and cut faces.

"We are now," Kenya responded.

"It was an old neighbor. He was always so nice us," Lizzie paused, "used to give us candy all the time when we were little."

"Looks like that changed some. Lotta that goin' 'round," Chuck said. "I had some good 'ol boys comin' 'round my place night 'fore last. I had muh family out to the barn; just Tommy was left, thick in the fever. They started a bangin' on muh door tryin' to get in an' hollerin' 'bout comin' in," Chuck paused reflectively for a bit. "They didn't make it off muh porch," he fiddled with the blob on the spit. "This duck's 'bout done. Want some?"

"I think we're gonna get going. We're out looking for my kids, maybe you've seen them? A set of twin eleven-year-old girls, a boy and another girl that are 8, a six-year-old girl and a dog. Have you seen them?" Lizzie asked hopefully.

"Cain't say as I have but I'll keep a look out for ya," Chuck responded.

"I've got some canned vegetables in my bag if you want them to go with your duck," Lizzie offered.

"That'd be mighty kind of ya. Thank you," Chuck smiled raising the sides of his mustache a touch.

Lizzie twisted her body so that her bag was facing Kenya. "Sweetie, can you grab him a couple of cans?"

Kenya rummaged through the bag pulling out a can of corn and one of French style string beans. Both cans had pull tops. She handed the cans to Chuck. He reached into his back pocket and pulled out a can opener on a string that was tied to a belt loop and then noticed the pull tops and let the can opener drop to the ground.

"Much obliged," he said as he pulled the top and placed one of the cans on the edge of the fire.

"If you should see them, my kids, could you tell them that I'm at their grandparent's house waiting for them?"

"I will. Good luck to y'all," he said standing and putting out his hand.

"Good luck to you," Lizzie said extending her hand to grab his, shook, and then walked down the sidewalk back to the street. Kenya copied Lizzie's words and actions and they were on their way.

The sky was showing signs of twilight starting to set in. Kenya pulled out her gun and her knife and she started carving something on the butt as she walked.

"Well, that was something you don't see every day," Lizzie commented as she surveyed the street ahead of them on their way back toward her parent's house.

"Um, I think we see a lot of stuff every day now that we've never seen before," Kenya responded while scratching with the tip of her knife. "Remember the elephant?"

"Right you are, my friend. Right you are," Lizzie noted.

There was silence between them with only the sound of metal scratching against hard plastic. Lizzie glanced over to see what Kenya was doing and could see the shape of a word forming.

"Whatcha doin' there, punkin?" Lizzie had been using more and more endearments with Kenya ever since the incident with Mr. Harvey.

"When you put down my friend, Amy, back when we met, I thought you killed her. You told me it was a mercy. I didn't really get it until now," she said with her head bowed to her task. "I'm carving the word, 'mercy' to remind myself what it actually means now."

The silence returned between them.

"Thank you," Kenya offered simply.

They had taken so many detours and wrong turns along the way to their grandparent's house. They were low on gas. They were low on food, as well. Low on hope of making it to their destination and high on fear of what roamed outside the confines of the minivan kept them moving.

"Guys, I think we're getting pretty close to Nana and Poppup's house. We are somewhere between Remington and Sumerduck," Lola said without looking up from her map.

"I'm hungry," Olivia said from her middle row booster seat.

"And I'm thirsty," Margaret chimed in from beside her.

Hershey panted loudly. The front seat windows were open and a breeze with an odor slightly tinged of smoke and death wafted through. It wasn't as bad here as it had been in the more populated areas they had driven through. Maybe the trees absorbed some of the stench.

"We're out of water," Mike said as he leaned over the back of the third-row seat, moved some bags around and rummaged through others. He grabbed a box, turned around and sat in his seat.

"We've just got this box of crackers. That's it; only three packages left."

"I've been looking for some place we could stop, a store or something and haven't seen anything," Lucy said.

"Take that left. It should get us back to seventeen," Lola directed.

"Stop!" Margaret yelled. "There's a store right there!"

It was a small house that had been converted into a little convenience store. There were wooden signs nailed to the front in between the windows advertising services and products that could be found inside. 'Fresh-cooked, made to order burgers!' and the exclamation point was excitedly exaggerated. There was another that listed bread, milk and farm-fresh eggs with a slate next to each where the price could be updated in chalk.

Lola parked the minivan parallel to the house and turned off the motor.

"Where's dad's wallet?" Lola asked. "I thought I had put it here in the console."

Lola and Lucy looked around the center console, moving things, pulling out papers, and a miniature crystal skull their mother had gotten at a yard sale.

"Did you check the floor?" Margaret asked.

Lola and Lucy checked around their feet. Lucy reached down under the seat and her hand hit on the leather pouch.

"Found it," Lucy announced. She opened the wallet and counted the dollar bills inside. "We have three hundred and seventy-five dollars. That's enough to get what we need for now."

They got out of the minivan, with four of the kids walking around the front of the vehicle. They walked up the three steps to the wooden porch that could use an updated paint job. In fact, the entire building could use an updated painted job. In some cases, needing a paint job or updating can add to the charm of a place but in this instance, the store fell far short of any kind of charm.

The door was open, and they slowly walked in. The store aisles were close together, with just enough room for one person to shop at a time.

"Stick with your Buckner Buddy," Mike reminded them.

"Hello? Is anyone here working?" Lucy yelled out.

There was no response.

"We can just leave money on the counter if there is no one here," Lucy said.

The paired-up girls moved about the store grabbing what food they could of what was left whole and not scattered and ripped open on the floor. Mike went to the front of the store with one gallon of water, the last drop of water that was left. He grabbed some plastic bags from behind the counter and went back to the coolers and pulled lukewarm sports drinks and soft drinks from the racks, doubling the bags and filling them to capacity. He made three trips to the front of the store.

"Hello?" Lola called facing the back of the store with Margaret by her side. They stood at the checkout counter, having placed their found goods on the counter. "Is anyone here? We want to check out."

"Why wouldn't anybody be here?" Margaret asked. "The door was open. They must be open. Someone should be working."

The girls stood at the counter looking toward the back of the store waiting for someone to appear to ring up their purchases. Mike joined them with an arm load of drinks and plopped them down on the counter. He walked around the back of the counter, grabbed some plastic bags and threw them across to the girls.

"Start bagging up the stuff you got," Mike ordered.

"But the guy hasn't rung them up yet. We can't," Margaret exclaimed.

"I don't think anyone is here," Lola said, somewhat sadly.

"We can't just take stuff. That's stealing! We'll get in trouble," Margaret retorted.

"I was thinking we could add it up, guesstimate how much and just leave the money on the counter," Mike offered to appease Margaret.

"Maybe we could leave a little extra just in case we figured it wrong," Margaret suggested.

They started stuffing their loot into the bags. Boxed donuts, cookies, cans of spaghetti, ravioli, soups and vegetables. Margaret had found a blueberry Bundt cake in a bakery box that she had salivated over a little bit. She planned to bite into that as soon as they got back into the minivan and hoped that she didn't have to share too much of it.

"C'mon Lucy and Olivia! Finish up so we can get out of here," Lola yelled without looking up.

Lucy and Olivia were near the back left of the store in the aisle with the cookies and crackers discussing the merits of Oreos.

"But don't you see? Once you scrape off the cream, you still have two cookies left. It's like the cream is the extra treat and scraping it off makes the whole thing last longer," Olivia pleaded her case.

"I don't care. I just want to shove the whole thing in my mouth and taste all the tastes at the same time," Lucy responded. "But you know, double stuff is good in theory but it's just on the wrong side of too much cream."

"You're right," Olivia agreed and then grabbed the five remaining bags of Oreos. "I'm done," she yelled out.

Lucy and Olivia started back up the aisle to join their siblings and check out. As they rounded the end of the aisle headed to the checkout counter, the backroom door popped open a smidge. Fingers curled around the door, gripping it. Something bumped against the door and there was a low, guttural groan of escaping breath with the essence of rotting corpse flavoring the air.

Lucy turned to see a mangled face in the shadow start to emerge. She screamed, surprised and shrill. She pushed Olivia to move her along and the girl fell face forward, arms extended in front of her splaying her stockpile of Oreo cookies across the floor.

"We gotta go!" Mike yelled seeing the meaty beast struggling to push its way through the backroom door. "Grab what you can and go get in the van!"

Mike ran around the corner carrying a bag of drink bottles. He dropped the bag at the door, bottles rolling in every direction, and pushed his sisters through the exit.

"Go!" He screamed. "Hurry!"

He turned and ran to Olivia, grabbed her by the scruff of her beach ball covered t-shirt. As if with a mysterious Herculean strength, he raised her to her feet with one hand and pushed her toward the door. She grabbed the one package of Oreos that was near the door as she went out.

The ogre had made it through the door and was struggling to advance toward the remaining Buckner kids. For some reason inexplicable to Mike, he stood transfixed by the visage of the thing. It was horribly mangled. One eye was completely missing, with just the bony remnants of the orbital socket dressed in meaty flesh. The remaining eye was swollen shut. It was an old man or at least, was dressed like one. He had a drab plaid button down shirt on with a worn out, holey V-necked cardigan and trousers. Every garment he wore was stained and crusty with blood. It slowly scraped its way toward them, its arms hanging useless, swaying slightly.

"Mike, we gotta go!" Lucy screamed hysterically as she bent to pick up one of the dropped Oreo packages.

"Forget about those," Mike screamed back pushing her along.

Lucy righted herself and took her next step, her foot landed on one of the drink bottles. The bottle pulled her leg forward causing Lucy to fall almost in a perfect split, but she crumbled at the last minute, screaming all the way down.

"Lucy! Lucy!" Mike screamed. "Lucy, I got you!"

Despite its slow, halted progress, the monstrosity that was once a storekeeper was almost upon the kids. The sudden and sharp pull on Lucy's adductor muscle hindered her in getting back up. She cringed in throbbing pain. Mike ran toward Lucy grabbing her beneath her arms and hoisted her as she pushed herself up still clutching the Oreos. Lucy reached the door, pushing it open and pulling Mike through with her. Mike stopped and pushed the door shut and braced himself against it, holding it closed.

"Go get the van running," he yelled over his shoulder. "I'll hold it off."

The ogre had reached the door and was doing its level best to force it open, but it was weak. It didn't take much effort for Mike to keep the door closed but he wasn't going to take any chances. He put all his strength in keeping that door closed until he could run for the minivan.

The thing pushed and smushed its face against the glass, streaking it with blood, the loose flesh dancing against it. Mike had to look down at his feet to keep himself from throwing up.

"Mike! C'mon! Let's go!" Lucy yelled from the driver's window.

Mike let go of the door and ran around the the minivan to the open side door and climbed in. Lucy floored the gas pedal. The van skidded wildly on some sand and then gained its footing once it hit the pavement of the road. Lucy's heart nearly beat out of her chest. They drove off as the ogre was still trying to make its way out of the store.

"Alright Lola, where are we going?" Lucy asked and handed Olivia the Oreos she'd grabbed only to see that Olivia had already ripped open the one package she managed to get out of the store with her.

Lola got them back on track and they'd been driving south about twenty minutes working their way back to route seventeen. Lola flipped down the visor so that she could look at the mirror. She powered her window down and grabbed one of the bags that she'd brought from the store. She pulled out a pair of scissors. Looking in the mirror, she brushed her fingers through her hair. She grabbed a tress of hair near the short tuft of hair that Mike had cut. She measured with her fingers and cut the length to match. She threw the cut hair out of the window and it floated off in the wind. She went back and continued with the cutting.

"Looks like you're going short, L," Lucy commented.

"What else am I going to do?" Lola responded and continued.

"Shit!" Lucy exclaimed looking at the road ahead.

"I'm writing that in my book and I'm going to tell Mommy you swore when we see her," Olivia informed Lucy.

"There's a huge accident up ahead guys. The entire road is blocked and then some," Lucy said observing the scene.

Mike was up from the back of the minivan in between the front bucket seats in less than a heartbeat.

"Looks like some people are wondering around," Lola said.

"Those aren't people," Mike responded. "Let's get out and see if we can see a way around this."

Lucy and Mike got out of the minivan, climbed up on the front the car and stood on the hood and surveyed the accident scene. A pickup truck was turned on its side blocking one lane and two cars had crashed into it. Debris from the cars, inside and out, lay spread across the road. A minibus that had tried to get around the mess had gotten wedged between one of the crashed cars and several trees. On the other side of the truck, the trees started within a foot of the road. Unless they walked, there was no way around the accident.

In and around the accident scene, five examples of the formerly living moved about aimlessly. There were four adults and one child. They didn't congregate, and they didn't follow one another in any direction. The child banged its fist against the window of one of the cars. The rest simply shuffled aimlessly.

"I think I see something moving in the car that the kid is banging on," Mike said.

"I think it's just one of them trapped in the car," Lucy answered. "I think we need to backtrack and find another way. We're so close and I don't want to go in the opposite direction away from Nana and Popup's."

"But we have to," Lola said.

Lucy climbed down from the hood as Mike jumped the distance from the hood to the ground, nearly landing on his knees.

Mike walked through the remainder of Lola's hair that she'd cut while the minivan had just been sitting there.

Lucy got back into the driver's seat and looked at Lola's new short haircut. Lola had managed to cut her entire head of hair almost all the same length, roughly about an inch in length all over her head. Some parts were longer, and some were shorter.

"I love it L," Lucy said staring at Lola's now very round head. "It really takes the attention away from your freckles."

"I don't have freckles."

"My point, exactly," Lucy said with a sympathetic smile. "Alright, how do we get around this?"

Lola grabbed her map book and ran her finger over the page looking for an answer.

Within twenty minutes, they were making their way down a somewhat narrow side road common to the area. Tree-lined so thick that at certain points, one could struggle to see the sky.

Lola looked over at the gas gauge and saw that it was hanging around at the quarter of a tank mark. She knew they were getting close; they'd been close most of today, but still hadn't made it to their grandparent's house.

"Hey Mike, any chance Dad put a jug of gas back there?" Lola asked hopefully, thinking that maybe he had, and they just hadn't seen it.

"Nope," Mike replied simply.

"I have to go to the bathroom," Olivia said.

"Me too," added Margaret.

"We probably all do," Lola chimed in.

"We can't waste any gas looking for a place so let's just use the woods," Lucy suggested.

Margaret balked.

"M, we've done it a million times camping with Dad! This is nothing new," Lucy said flatly.

"I'd say all of this is new," Mike commented.

Lucy pulled the minivan over to the side of the road and came to a stop. They all lumbered out, Hershey nearly trampling Mike as he bounded through the sliding door. The dog took a few steps, lifted his leg and found some badly needed relief. Once he was done, he started his sniffing inspection of the area all the while keeping his eyes on his kids.

"You guys go," Mike said, "Hershey and me will watch from here."

"Don't look at me!" Olivia yelled.

"You know what I mean, O," Mike yelled back defensively.

Lucy and Olivia, Lola and Margaret walked across the street in pairs and then each pair disappeared into the thick foliage that lined the country road like spectators at a parade. When the girls could mostly be heard and not seen, Mike went to the back of the minivan and did his business with privacy while keeping an eye on the area his sisters had disappeared into.

Mike finished and came around to the side of the minivan facing the street. Leaning back against the van, he could hear his sisters bicker and laugh while leaves and branches shook like they were dancing as the girls moved around.

The weather was warm and the afternoon fine, perfect in fact, for a game of baseball or hide and seek but there was no time for that. He was worried about their need for gas and the service stations they'd stopped at not being operable.

Mike looked down the country road to left and then to his right. Birds chirping, the sound of leaves bristling on the breeze, peaceful except for his sisters yammering away.

To Mike's right, there was the shaking of bushes and Hershey launched into a barrage of suspicious barking while advancing toward the unknown cause of the sounds.

Mike yelled for his sisters to hurry and return to the van as he advanced across the street toward the girls to move them along.

Hershey crossed Mike's path and stopped in the street, hackles up and growling. Between the trees and out of the bushes came a man wearing an olive-green fishing hat, hip boots and an unlit cigarette dangling from his mouth. In one hand he carried a fishing pole and in the other a string of fish that he'd caught. In a hushed voice loud enough to be heard, the man begged Mike to call off the dog. Mike rushed to the dog, grabbed his collar and soothed Hershey.

"Sssh, it's alright boy," Mike whispered into Hershey's ear while he rubbed the dog's midsection roughly.

"There's man-eaters out here for chri-sakes. No need to tell 'em where dinner's at," the man scowled and leaned over to put his hand within sniffing distance of Hershey's nose. Hershey acquiesced and the man reached out and rubbed the dog's head.

"Sorry. He's just looking out for us."

"Good boy," the man said as he continued patting the dog.

The girls approached closing in around Mike and Hershey and stared curiously at the man.

"What're you kids doing out here? Where's your mom, dad?"

"Our mom is meeting us at our grandparent's house in Hartwood," Lola answered.

"Our dad didn't make it," Mike added looking down at his feet.

"Yeah," the man said sighing, "lotta that goin' 'round these days."

The kids and dog stared at the man. The man stared back at them.

"Name's Thaddeus," the man said breaking the silence.

"I'm Mike. That's Lola, Lucy, she's the oldest. That's Margaret and Olivia, she's the youngest," Mike introduced his sisters pointing at each as he went.

"Mr. Thaddeus-,"

"Thaddeus. Just Thaddeus."

"Thaddeus," Lucy started again, "we really need some gas. I don't think we have enough to get to our grandparent's house. Can you help us?"

"I think so. Got 'nything for trade?"

"Like money? We got some money," Lola said.

"Maybe, but that's about near worthless at this moment in time. Got 'nything else?"

"Gatorade?" Olivia asked. "Everybody likes Gatorade."

"Ya getting' warmer there. Mind if I take a look in the back of your van and see whatcha gut?" Thaddeus said as he walked over to the back of the van and threw up the liftgate and started rooting through around and muttering to himself. Olivia chased after him worried that he might spot and want her Oreos. The kids soon joined him and watched as he moved things around, sorting through what they had. His hand wrapped around a box and he turned, shaking it in his hand at them.

"See what this is?" He asked holding the box up for the kids to see and shook it again. "This! This is the new currency, shotgun shells."

"We don't even have a shotgun," Mike said.

"Maybe not but it'll get you five gallons of gas for this box."

"Ten," Lucy countered.

"Now don't get greedy," Thaddeus responded.

Down a long driveway that was heavily camouflaged from the street, sat Thaddeus' small house and large barn. Lush greenery nearly enveloped the house and crops stretched out behind the barn.

He disappeared into his barn for a prolonged period before he reappeared carrying a jug of gas and a plastic funnel.

Thaddeus walked to the van talking all the way about how it was just a matter of time before the world went to hell in a handbasket and now that it had, he was more than ready for it. Yessiree, he was ready.

"How'd you know?" Olivia asked standing behind and watching his progress.

"Just did. Grew up knowin' it, maybe. You know it?"

"Not really. I don't know much of anything yet. I'm only six, so far," Olivia responded.

"Guess you've seen it firsthand then. Better pay 'tention and be careful or you'll never see seven," Thaddeus advised.

Thaddeus tipped the gas can up as far as it would go, gave it a final tap and then screwed the cap back on.

"Alright now, you kids is ready to go."

"Thaddeus," Lola said walking over to him with the closed map book, "can you tell us how to get back to route seventeen? Our grandparents live near there."

"Down the end of," he said, stopped and thought, "I gotta go back down there with ya and make sure my gate is closed up good, so no one knows that I'm down here."

At the end of the driveway, Thaddeus jumped out of the van and opened the gate. Lucy pulled the minivan through the threshold and stopped. Lola looked back at him and asked which way to go.

"Take a right out of the driveway. At the end of this street, it'll be a T-intersection, go right. That'll getchas back to sev'teen.

Good luck to yas and stay away from those man-eaters!" He said and banged the roof of the minivan.

Lucy pulled slowly back onto the country road, turning right as instructed. At the T-intersection, she turned left.

Cluttered Remains of Survival

Ten minutes down a road that was a wrong turn from the beginning, a piece of wood with one nail hammered through one side, sticking out three inches the other side, lay on the pointy side up. Dried blood coated the end of the board impaled with the nail. Lucy, an inexperienced driver, drove over the board. It slapped up against the side panel of the minivan, flipped and then pierced the rear passenger wheel and then spun away. The customary thump, thump, thump swan song of a flattened tire serenaded the kids.

"What's wrong with the van?" Lucy yelled. "It's pulling to the right!"

Lucy braked to slow the van and hoped that she'd regain control.

"Flat tire, Einstein," Mike shouted. "Pull over somewhere and we'll change it."

"I gotta pee, anyway," Margaret said.

"We just stopped for that not too long ago," Lucy responded.

They had been driving for almost twenty-five minutes in the wrong direction without realizing it.

"I drank a whole blue Gatorade really fast and now it wants out," Margaret explained.

"I need a chance to find out where we are anyway. I haven't seen any of the streets marked on the map," Lola said.

The GPS had stopped working at some point today. Lola wasn't sure when it went blank but just knew that it had.

Lucy stopped the minivan on the side of the road in front of a side yard where dandelions and weeds stretched above the overgrown grass that was trying to catch up in the race toward the sun's rays of light.

All the doors opened, and the Buckner kids spilled out with Hershey being the first to put paws on the ground.

Margaret wondered off behind some bushes near a blue house set back from the street. Mike immediately went to examine the flat tire. He looked at its pathetic, deflated state of being. He kicked the dead tire, not out of frustration, but because he thought that was the thing to do.

"Mike? Gonna help us?" Lola yelled from the back of the minivan where she and Lucy had the gate lifted and were pulling out all the bags and boxes to get to the spare tire.

"Put the go-bags to the side so we put them back in last. I think the spare and jack is in the cubby under all this stuff," Lucy said pulling out a box and putting it to the side. "Olivia," she yelled, "stay close if you're not going to help."

"Find the lug wrench yet?" Mike asked squeezing between Lucy and Lola to look for himself.

Lola pulled out some bags so that Mike could lift the lid to the spare tire compartment. He reached in and pulled out the lug wrench and twirled the four-pronged instrument between his fingers as he walked back around to the flat tire. He knelt and slipped the lug wrench onto one of the lug nuts and began his struggle.

"O, come here and grab the jack, will ya?" Lola asked. "Bring it to Mike."

Olivia took the jack from Lola's hand and walked it around to Mike. Lucy and Lola pulled, shifted and tugged until they got the spare tire out of the compartment. Instead of just a doughnut tire, their Dad had put in a full-sized tire.

Lucy started reorganizing their cargo, readying it for reloading once the tire was changed.

"Here you go, M," Lola said as she rolled the tire to the side of the minivan.

Mike was jumping on the lug wrench like he was trying to kick start a motorcycle, trying his hardest to loosen the lug nuts but they just wouldn't budge.

"These fuckers are on tight." Mike groaned.

"Good thing Olivia didn't hear that," Lola replied.

"I heard it!" Olivia yelled from the front lawn where she was playing with Hershey. "I'm givin' Mike a freebie!"

"L, can you push that side down while I pull up on the other side?" Mike asked Lola, pointing to the spoke of the four-sided lug wrench. "On three. Ready?"

Both the kids grabbed their respective side of the lug wrench and got ready to push or pull. Mike counted one, counted two and just as he said three, hysterical screaming came from the bushes toward the back of the house they were stopped in front of. It was Margaret.

The four Buckner kids and Hershey raced across the lawn toward Margaret's screaming. Mike in a sprint with the lug wrench in his hand. Lucy having grabbed the baseball bat her father had packed before she took off running and screamed at Lola to stay back and get Olivia into the minivan. Hershey, faster than any cheetah that ever lived, barked ferociously with a blood-thirsty growl warning whatever waited for him that upon his arrival, he would have to be dealt with.

When Mike arrived, Margaret cowered frozen in place crouched on the ground. She screamed like a wild banshee as a cannibal animal approached. Mike grabbed Margaret by the shoulder and threw her away from the oncoming monster. She landed face down with her pants at her ankles, her bare behind greeting the world for the first time since picture time at the portrait studio when she was born.

Mike continued forward meeting the one-minded numbskull before it got to Margaret. The stench of death, feces and whatever smells like that should have caused Mike to shudder but it didn't. He was impervious to anything that would take the focus off saving his twin. Mike swung his arm, beating the bag of necrotic flesh with the four-sided lug wrench but it didn't seem to care.

Lucy arrived and grabbed Margaret, helping her to her feet. Both girls grabbed at Margaret's pants. Lucy was trying to keep Margaret upright and moving. Margaret, despite being terrified, was also acutely aware of her nakedness and her need to cover up.

"Hurry up! Get the fuck out of here!" Mike screamed as he swung away and batted off hands before they took hold. Hershey danced around the monstrosity, barked and tried to knock it off balance.

Lucy gave the back of Margaret's pants a hard yank and got the girl running with an atomic wedge firmly in place.

"I don't know how much longer I can fight it off," Mike said looking away to see the girls run. But that's all it took.

It lunged at Mike. Hershey pushed it from behind. It fell upon Mike, knocked the boy down and then fell on top of him. Mike desperately turned his body to crawl out from underneath just as teeth ripped into his thigh. It ripped the denim of Mike's jeans along with pulling flesh from the bone. A geyser of blood spurted out in hysterical surges once the femoral artery was severed.

Mike, twisted on his stomach, screamed in pain and for the girls to run, to leave him. Hershey didn't let up. He pounced, nipped, bit and ripped at the ghoul to get its attention. It would look at him, chew, then look back down. The dog wouldn't stop.

It took another bite from Mike's leg. Mike wasn't screaming. Mike wasn't moving. It looked up and its head met the wallop of a baseball bat cracking the cranial bones that would no longer protect the writhing, wormy brain squarely encased within. The thing fell over as the animation left its being. Its blood, cranial bone and gray matter spilled out of the cracks created when Lucy wielded the bat.

Lucy dropped the bat. She picked up Mike and pulled him out from underneath the thing that killed him. She fell hard backward to the soft grass and pulled Mike onto her lap and cradled him. Lola, Margaret and Olivia ran up and fell about them, crying in disbelief. Each sister reached out to touch him and hold on to each other. Hershey nosed his way in, lay down with his snout on Mike's bloodied legs.

Lucy's tears fell into Mike's red hair mixing with blood that had sprayed into it, had coated the tufts of soft red curls and scalp, dripping onto his face. Lola tried to wipe blood from his face, but it was of no use. Olivia cried his name over and over again, begging him to wake up. Margaret just stared through her tears whispering incoherently.

A breath escaped his lips. The girls stopped breathing. His eyes opened and he looked at his sisters and he smiled. His eyes closed. That was it. Mike was gone.

The girls cried harder, huddled around his body. Hershey let out a low wail that came from deep within his gut. They sat in their grief, ignorant of what they should do next.

Hershey started growling, fur raised up on his back. He looked to the backyard where they all saw that two more of these creatures slowly ambled toward the huddled group. They came across from the yard that abutted up against the one that they were in. They responded to Hershey's warning with their own growls and moans.

"We have to go," Lucy said quietly. "We have to go."

"We can't leave him," Margaret said desperately.

"We can't take him. He will become one of those," Lola said with half a gulp.

"We can't let him," Margaret said.

"I can't do it. Can you?" Lola asked.

"Doesn't matter. We gotta go now," Lucy said with flat urgency. She slowly rolled out from under Mike, laying him gently on the ground. She knelt beside him and kissed his forehead. "I love you, Mike."

Lucy got up and Lola took her place, kissing Mike's forehead saying, "You were always my favorite brother, M."

"C'mon O. We gotta go," Lucy said lightly touching Olivia's back trying to urge her to move.

Olivia fell upon Mike and sobbed heavily. Lucy bent and picked her up and carried her to the minivan.

Hershey ran from the girls toward the approaching threat. His barking ramped up; it had gone to a deep, dark scary place in hopes that he'd scare the predators off. He soon growled in the distance, just out of view.

Lola put her hand on Margaret's back and looked down at her.

"We have to go now. Now!" Lola said firmly in a soft voice.

"I know," Margaret said. "This isn't it for us." She grabbed the bloodied bat and got to her feet.

The two girls walked quickly to the minivan and arrived just after Lucy put Olivia down.

"Grab your go-bag and let's go," Lucy instructed.

They each grabbed their backpack putting it on as they walked. Lucy grabbed Mike's and slung it over one shoulder, it bounced off her backpack strapped to her back. She grabbed Olivia's hand and pulled the sobbing child along.

Hershey's barks rose an octave and then stopped with a sharp cry of pain.

"Hershey!" Olivia screamed and pulled toward the sound.

"We can't, O. We have to get out of here. It sucks but we do," Lucy said and continued to pull the girl along.

They all cried but only Margaret could be heard. Lola supported and pulled her sister along as they all walked quickly away. The family dog having bought them some traveling time with his sacrifice.

"Sandrine! Sandrine! Quick! Do what I say, now!" The woman said with urgency.

"Mama, what's wrong?" Sandrine asked looking wildly about the car.

The woman quickly got out of the car and opened the backseat passenger door in one fluid movement. She furiously pulled items from the backseat and threw them carelessly on the road.

Mother and daughter had been on the road for five days already trying to get back home to Virginia, south of Richmond. They'd been in a teeny, tiny town in Pennsylvania called Georgetown visiting with Sandrine's grandparents. They'd had a lovely visit and had left as planned. Things went south a day after they had started for home. Sandrine's mother would never had left if she'd known that catastrophe and disaster would be unfolding everywhere. Her repeated attempts to turn around and go back to her parents were constantly thwarted and detoured until they were so far along there was no other course but to continue forward.

Moving from one variety of roadblock to another, they were now in a long line on the side of a Virginia road waiting to get into a refugee camp. A sloping embankment rolled down on their left, evened out with the road that they were on and then sloped down on the right rolling right into a big field bordered by trees on all sides.

Soldiers had come through the line to hand out MRE's, water and to collect information, always promising that they would be admitted very soon. Meanwhile, large convoy vehicles would loudly drive by in both directions, shaking the ground beneath as they went. Bursts of gunshots would periodically sound.

Sandrine's mother had been reading aloud from a battered copy of Charlotte's Web which worked well to distract Sandrine and it helped to keep her from crying out hysterically and instead enabled her to keep it in as a continual internal crying jag. As she turned the page to a new chapter, she heard one long, resounding scream ascending to the trees above. She glimpsed what was coming for them as that one scream fractured into many.

"Hurry! You've got to get into the trunk," the woman yelled as she pressed the button that released the backseat, opening to a dark storage hold.

Sandrine stared at her mother, hearing nothing, blank-faced and frozen in her seat.

Chaos was climbing to ever higher heights all around them. Gunfire, single shot and automatic rang out. Screams came from every direction along with the people issuing them. Metal slammed into metal up ahead while the panic level grew greater with each passing second.

"Now, damn it!" Her mother screeched. "Hurry!"

Sandrine suddenly snapped back into motion but the world, for her was still silent. She scrambled to the back climbing between the two front bucket seats and across the folded down backseat. She slid her lower body through the hole, twisting to rest on her hands and knees looking up at her mother with wide, terrified eyes.

"I'll be back for you," her mother promised, bending to kiss her daughter's head, lingering a moment.

When her mother pulled away, the world exploded in the most horrifying sounds she'd ever heard. Every imaginable, horrific sound of terror crashed together at once in sheer pandemonium.

"Scoot back," her mother said.

Sandrine backed into the dark compartment and wrapped her arms around her knees. The woman snapped the seat back into place, turned and then her screaming began. Sandrine heard her mother's body being thrown against the car, excited growls and flesh being ripped from the bone and her mother shrieking in response.

So many sounds converged upon Sandrine's ears that she could no longer discern her mother's cries from any of the others. Car wheels squealing, people howling, horns blaring, the sounds of vehicles crashing into things and each other and then for hours there were moans, groans, growls and an occasional scream. At one point, a man screamed out in such heinous agony for what seemed an eternity at the back of the car, right outside the trunk that Sandrine was concealed in. In the near distance, there had been the sound of a baby crying that stopped abruptly. She knew what that meant but she preferred to think otherwise.

Eventually, the shrieks shrank to moans that were drowned out by noises that the monsters made as they ate and moved on. Then there was silence. Sandrine banged against the backseat trying to open it so that she could go to her mother, but it was of no use. She was locked in. Hours passed. Silence largely returned. Sandrine rolled over into a fetal ball, the soft skin of her cheek resting against the rough carpet of the trunk. She slept.

She woke to the sound and feeling of someone getting into the front seat of the car. She looked toward the noise, listening for anything that might tell her what had gotten in. She heard a male voice talking but no one answered. Was he alone?

"Oh, thank God!" Sandrine heard him exclaim after hearing the keys jingle and the engine turn over and start. Then the door closed. The car shifted into drive and started moving.

Sandrine banged her hands against the back of the seat. She couldn't bear being trapped in the trunk any longer. The car stopped, jerked into park.

"What the fuck was that?" The male voice asked followed by silence as he listened for more to determine the cause of the noise.

Sandrine banged again on the back of the seat and started begging to be let out.

She heard the car door open and then slow footsteps, soles softly grinding against the pebbles and sand on the road. The backseat door opened. There was silence. The pop of the release button and then the seat slowly being pulled back. Day light jarringly filtered into the dark trunk. Sandrine was blinded. When her eyes adjusted, they looked into the barrel of a gun. Sandrine cried.

"No, no, no. Please don't cry. I'm not going to hurt you," he said, lowering the gun and stuffing it into the waistband of his pants, and he put out his hand. "C'mon. Come on out of there."

Sandrine inched forward hesitant to leave the safety of the trunk but anxious to get out of the hot box that the trunk had become just the same.

"That's it. I'm not gonna hurt you. My name is Lucas, Lucas Dodge, to be exact," he said softly still extending his hand. "What's your name?"

"Sandrine Dumont," she replied as she swept a strand of her brown hair out of her eyes and behind her ear. She reached out and grabbed his hand.

Lucas pulled her out and remarked at how light she was.

"How old are you, sweetheart?" Lucas asked.

"I'm six and a half. How old are you?" She asked in return while she jumped down from the backseat of the car and onto the street.

"Well, I guess I am twenty-three and half. Are you here alo-," he stopped short looking past the girl to blobs of scattered human flesh that was spread about the road near where he'd found the car. And then it hit him, a girl alone locked in the trunk, a pile of bloody flesh and blood covered clothes belonging to a woman scattered not far away; this was likely the girl's mother.

"Shit," he said softly to himself.

"What?" she asked confused.

"Sorry, Sandrine. I was just thinking out loud."

"Have you seen my mama? I think she's hurt."

"She is. Pretty badly. They got her. How about you come with me?"

She looked at him blankly.

"You've got a car and can't drive. I can drive but don't have a car. I think we'd make a great team. What do you think?"

"Okay," she answered after a moment of processing the thoughts of what had likely become of her mother.

She walked around the open backseat door and scrambled across the driver's side and buckled herself into the passenger seat. He got in beside her, started the car and shifted into drive.

"You forgot to buckle your seatbelt," she reminded him.

"Ya know, you're right. Thanks for reminding me," he said smiling and reaching around to find the belt and put it on.

"Where are we going?"

"I dunno. Out of here if we can. Know where we are?"

"No. I don't think so. I don't really know where we are. Me and my mama were at Grammy and Grampy's house visiting and then we were going home and got stuck here."

They were moving slowly, driving over all sorts of stuff in the road, slaloming between it all. Along the side of the road to the right were the cars that remained from waiting to enter the refugee camp. The closer they got to the entrance to the camp, the harder it was to move through a panic that would never go down in the history books.

The entrance was nothing but a mash up of vehicles. With the oncoming hoard, people drove straight at the gate, converging all at once with no care about what was in front of them. The goal was to get behind the gates, get to safety. Instead, the gates were run down and no one made it. Bodies, pieces of bodies, parts of vehicles, anything that could be thrown free was distributed in a life-sized Rorschach test of blood, guts and the remnants of humanity.

"Sit tight for sec, okay? I need to see if there's a way to get the car through," Lucas said.

Sandrine looked up at him and nodded.

Lucas got out of the car and stood looking for a moment, leaning one way and then the other. The left side of the road was at the bottom of a steep hill of heavy brush and foliage. The right side was lined in hastily put up cyclone fencing with the ground in a steep drop on the other side of it, down into the field littered in tents of all sizes, some still erect and some collapsed. Dead people of all condition lay everywhere in every position. Vehicles and equipment spread out randomly having lost the sense of order a military camp would have.

Climbing up onto the bed of a truck to get a look from higher ground, Lucas looked for a way through this flesh and metal melee with a car. He finally concluded that they would have to make their way through on foot. He scanned the area for any remaining animated corpses and saw nothing he didn't think he could handle. He could see some of the dead fighting to get out of cars that they were trapped in. Way in the distance he saw two moving away from all of this. No matter how hard he looked, he could see nothing still alive.

He went back to the car, slid into the driver's seat, leaving one foot still planted on the road. Turning to look at Sandrine he said, "From what I saw, it looks like the road up ahead clears up some which is good news," he stopped, took a breath and continued, "but there's no way we're going to get this car through that junkpile of cars in front of us. It's just too much, there's too much. We're going to have to walk through all of that and find another car on the other side."

Sandrine looked at Lucas with an *I'm about to cry but I really don't want to and I'm really scared* face.

"Oh, no, no," Lucas said panicking. He did not know what to do with a crying little girl having no experience with such.

But that was it. She burst out in hard tears. She was overdue, really, not having dropped one tear since this had all begun, not even when she was locked into the trunk and her mother was being ripped to shreds on the other side of the fiberglass fender.

And that was it. Lucas broke down. It started as a cough and rolled into a deep, resounding guttural wail. He bent over, head against the steering wheel and wept. He'd kept his wits about him from the beginning. He was strong when his mother told him that his father had been bit and turned. He was strong when she called and told him his brother had not come home from baseball practice and she hadn't heard from him. He was strong when he said good-bye to her, heard her last breath and upon leaving the phone line open, her first snarl.

Lucas' tears stopped Sandrine's. She had never seen a grown man cry. She didn't know that they could.

"Lucas," she said while wiping her face and eyes, "please don't cry. I won't cry anymore if you don't."

He lifted his head and looked into her giant brown eyes, her face so open and innocent and got hold of himself.

"I'm so sorry," Lucas said rubbing his wet, red-blotched face. "It all just hit me, you know?"

"Uh, huh," she responded, nodding slowly. She looked through the windshield, seeing the demolition of her world in front of her. "My mama is dead."

"I know. Mine is too."

They sat in silence looking out the windows taking in everything that was and wasn't happening around them.

"Well," Lucas finally said, "we need to get moving. We can't stay here."

"I'm scared," Sandrine whispered.

"Know what? Me, too," he sighed. "But you know what? We're going to be okay. You know why?"

"Why?"

"Because you and me? We are invincible."

"They can't see us?" She asked.

Lucas chuckled. "No, sweetie. We are invincible which means those monsters need to watch out for us 'cause we are trouble. Those things don't stand a chance against us. We are like our own kind of superheroes."

"Really?" Sandrine asked, praying it was true.

"Really. And I can tell that you are such a bad ass that whatever is on the other side needs to watch out for you!"

"Really?"

"Oh, yeah. That's what I think," Lucas said reaching down to grab his backpack. "You got a backpack or something?"

"Yeah, my school one but it has my stuff in it now."

They slowly picked their way through the piled up, mangled wreckage. A couple of times they had to climb up, across and over several heaps of mashed up plastic and metal.

They stood on the bed of a truck whose contents had been thrown all over with all the impacts from other vehicles it had experienced. In front of them, the undercarriage of a car turned on its side presented the next obstacle.

Lucas lifted Sandrine up, placing her atop the passenger door of the car and threw her bag up after her. Sandrine stood and looked out at the road carpeted with the discarded cluttered remnants of survival much the same she would a beautiful field of wildflowers, with awe.

"There's a bunch of smashed up cars on this side," Sandrine said in wonderment as Lucas came to stand beside her.

The occupants of the car on which they were perched, came alive, reaching for them, reaching for delectable sustenance barred from them by closed glass windows.

"This actually looks like it could be fun," Lucas said looking out over the newly minted junkyard with a smile. "We can run over the tops of the cars like it's an obstacle course."

"It does look like fun!"

"Ready? I'll lower you down but wait 'til I get down there before you go anywhere. Okay?"

Sandrine nodded her understanding. She turned, he grabbed her hands and carefully lowered her to the crinkled hood of the car below them and handed down her backpack. He told her to put it on and be ready go as he slid down beside her.

"Follow me," he said as he ran over the roof of that first car and onto the trunk and over to the next.

Through the crowded, smashed up metal phalanx, they made their way. Sometimes, dodging bloodied hands reaching out through broken glass and staying ahead of the few cannibal animals that had freed themselves from their motored traps or had been left behind by the herd that had passed through earlier.

They cleared the last of the car bridge and returned to traveling directly on the road once again. They went from car to car looking for an empty one with the keys inside and had no luck. The sad, bloodied and seemingly blank-staring faces looking back at them from behind windows sealing them into their unexpected burial tombs scared and saddened the pair.

One of the last cars, fourth from the end, a late model blue Chevy sedan finally answered Lucas' silent prayer.

Sandrine stood in the street watching a monster slowly pick its way toward them, oh so slowly, through the metal maze about three hundred feet away. Despite feeling panicked, she did not want to betray the fear she felt to Lucas. Instead, she just watched with eyes as big as pie plates full of concern. She trusted Lucas. They were invincible, after all.

Lucas peered in through the driver's side window, checking for any signs of former life and saw none in either the front or back seats. He reached around the steering wheel and felt the ring of keys in the ignition and let out a sigh of relief. As he was pulling his upper body out of the car, he saw it.

"Stay here for a second," he said to Sandrine. He walked around the car, taking sidesteps between its bumper and the bumper of the truck behind the Chevy to get to the other side and the back-passenger door.

Lucas opened the door, broken glass falling and tinkling. He looked at the empty, save for a tiny stuffed animal, blood-covered baby car seat. He reached in and tried to pull it out but realized that it was buckled to the backseat of the car. He yelled to Sandrine asking if she was okay while he worked at freeing the seat. He pulled the seat out and dropped it to the ground. There was some blood on the backseat. He grabbed a small blanket, wiped at it the best that he could but only got the stain down to a smear.

"Sandrine, climb in on the driver's side," he directed her, dropping the blanket on the ground and closing the door. He slid over the back of the trunk wondering why he hadn't done that before.

"We are going to have some fun backing this mofo boat out of here. Least no one will be looking for a note with my insurance info."

"What's a mofo?"

"A pain in the butt something or other and something you shouldn't be saying," he said more to admonish himself for using poor language in front of a little girl than to explain what he said to her.

"Who's going to care?" Sandrine said with more poignancy than either of them realized was there.

"I do," Lucas said turning the key in the ignition. "I care."

Sandrine looked at him and gave him a tiny smile.

There was more play in front of the Chevy sedan than there was behind it. Lucas cut the wheel as far to the left as he could and pulled forward slowly pushing into the Mini Cooper in front of them. With his foot firmly on the brake, hoping to not to lose any ground he cut the wheel all the way to the right and backed up as much as he could, crunching the tail of the car into the grill of the truck.

In four cycles of cutting the wheel, inching forward and back, they were out. Lucas had the car turned around and ready to go.

Lucas looked in the rearview mirror and saw a few advancing stragglers.

"Shit! I wanted to look through some of these cars for supplies but we're not going to have time with those Z's coming and with that broken window in the back."

"What are Z's?" Sandrine asked.

"Zombies. You know, mindless idiots like those dead things walking around," he explained.

"Oh," came her simple response. "I've never heard that before."

Two had gotten close to the back of the car. He put the car in reverse, looking in the rearview as he ploughed over them.

"Two less looking to be seated for dinner tonight," he said sarcastically. He shifted the car into drive and floored the gas pedal. The rear tires skidded on the gore at first but soon found purchase against drier pavement. They raced down the country lane.

"You're really committed to keeping your hair free of gunk wearing a knitted hat in weather like this," Lizzie commented on Kenya's headwear.

"It's worth it to me to not get anything mixed up with my hair."

They were driving, out looking for the kids and supplies. Kenya had been sharing her love of high school dating gossip. She hadn't been much of a participant since her former life consisted mostly of working and studying. However, that didn't stop her from having had a major crush on a boy in her math class. She had been hoping that he would get her telepathic messages to ask her to the senior prom, but time on that life ran out.

"In a way, I'm kind of glad that I haven't had to deal with dating yet," Kenya said.

"Why not?"

"Well, one, since no one will ever date again in human history I won't have to worry about what I'm missing and two? Well, two is a bit embarrassing and it makes a lot of sense that it's number two. I'm kinda gassy," Kenya confessed sheepishly. "I have been known to commit random acts of unexpected flatulence many, many times at the worst possible moment."

Lizzie burst out laughing.

"There was this one time when I was giving an oral report on Ptolemy in math class," she trailed off and thought for a second.

Lizzie was laughing so hard at the thought of poor Kenya up in front of her class reporting on someone she had never heard of and just snorted which made her laugh harder.

As if Kenya didn't notice the raucous laughter she continued, "but now that I think of it, I can't remember the last time that happened," Kenya said in wonderment to Lizzie's hysterical laughter. "Maybe it has to do with eating crackers and stuff that comes out of cans?

"If anything, I think food coming from cans would make you toot even more," Lizzie said squeezing out the words between chortles.

"Toot! You said toot," Kenya said and then snorted laughter.

"It just sounds better than fart," Lizzie said laughingly but then abruptly floored the gas pedal until stopping short behind a minivan.

"What's wrong? What are you doing?" Kenya yelled as her head whipped forward and then back.

"That looks like my minivan," Lizzie replied as she jumped out of the car and ran to the van. The lift gate was open. Lizzie reached up and pulled it down to see the license plate: it read "Buck

1." Her face was at first sheer elation and then it quickly plummeted to frantic concern as she rushed to the driver's door with Kenya chasing after her carefully picking her way through the minivan's contents that had been strewn about the outside and around the van. "This is my car! Where are they?" She yelled as she opened the door.

Lizzie leaned in and saw food wrappers on the floor and that the keys were still in the ignition. She got in and turned the ignition and saw that there was gas. If not the gas, then what happened? She looked at Kenya with a quizzical, thoughtful face.

"Where are they?" Lizzie said looking at Kenya. "There's gas in the tank. What happened?" She asked pulling the keys from the ignition.

"I don't know," Kenya answered and turned to walk to the back of the van with Lizzie following.

They stood at the back of the van. Lizzie looked to a blue house, set back from the street. The lawn was overgrown and dotted with dandelions growing with reckless abandon since no mower was regularly beating them back. A soft breeze swept across the tops of the trees but nothing else moved.

Kenya walked around Lizzie to the passenger side of the van and saw the flat tire.

"Well, mystery solved. Tire's flat. That's why they stopped," Kenya said.

"Okay, then, where are they?" Lizzie wondered aloud, looking around. She put the keys into the big pocket on her coat and heard them hit her gun. "Lucy!" She screamed. "Lola! Mike! Margaret! Olivia!" Lizzie turned and looked in all the directions for any kind of response, but none came.

Lizzie walked to back of the van again. She knelt on one knee in front of a box and opened it while Kenya came around beside her and started to sift through things. Inside the box was the book that Lizzie had told Lucy to get. She opened the book to reveal that instead of pages as expected it was actually a hollowed-out space concealing a gun and some loose bullets.

"Where are they?" Lizzie said as much to herself as to Kenya.

"We should take some of this stuff with us. What's that?"

Lizzie lifted the gun from out of the book and turned it over in her hand, the nickel finish glinting in the sun. "This was my father's. His father gave it to him when he went off to Vietnam. After my father didn't have any sons, he gave it to Kevin as a wedding gift to his first son-in-law. This is a .357 Magnum Colt Python." She looked at the gun thoughtfully. "I have heard about this gun my whole life, but this is the first time I've ever held it without my father or Kevin being right next to me."

"Seriously? I guess you finally have the balls required to hold it all by yourself," Kenya sarcastically responded walking toward the car with some of the salvaged items.

"Yeah, right," Lizzie nodded her head in agreement and put the gun back into the box as the ammunition rolled around. She heard a gurgle and a hiss. Lizzie looked up to see Mike walk around the back-end corner of the minivan. Mike's mouth was caked in blood, some dried, some glistening wet.

Mike advanced slowly, a troubled gait, dragging his leg. The thigh of his jeans ripped open from hip to knee, a flap of muscle hung over the knee. If the waistband of the jeans were not still hugging his hips, his torn pants would have tripped him already. His dead, glazed eyes oozed puss that mixed with rivulets of blood.

Mike's eyes offered no glimmer of recognition at the sight of his mother.

Mike carried in one hand something black, furry and bloody.

"What is that in his hand?" Kenya asked. "Is it some kind of animal?"

Lizzie looked at it. It wasn't very long and it was covered in short, black fur that came to a point on one end and bloody and revealing bone on the other.

"Could it be a tail or something like that?" Kenya ventured.

"I think so," Lizzie said. She realized that they hadn't seen or heard Hershey.

As Mike got closer to his mother, he lifted the arm that was carrying the black, furry object in front of him, his hand dropping its contents to the ground. Lizzie realized that it was very likely Hershey's tail. Her face crumpled up, her cheeks forcing her eyes to squeeze out projectile tears. She dropped the book into the box below it and stretched her arms out to Mike. Mike continued on a direct path with every intention of falling into Lizzie's arms. Lizzie kept repeating, "No. Mike, no," over and over through her anguished sobs.

"Lizzie, you can't!" Kenya yelled as she walked up to Mike and put Dan's gun with the "mercy" inscribed grip against Mike's temple and pulled the trigger. Mike dropped to the ground as if no longer being held up by puppet strings. Lizzie lunged after Mike to break his fall but didn't get there in time.

Mike's mother picked up her only son's body and pulled him close. The boy's head rolled back away from his mother as if he was repulsed by Lizzie's embrace. Lizzie shifted Mike's body so that she cradled the boy. She looked down into her baby's bloody, dead and puffy face with the open vitreous, blinded eyes, puss seeping from them. No recognition. None. There never would be again.

Lizzie saw her precious infant with a shocking puff of loosely curled, red hair, so thick and full that it seemed to radiate from his head. He had the brilliant blue eyes of a newborn with the wisdom of an old soul looking back at her.

She saw Kevin holding Mike for the first time, bathed by moonlight coming through a hospital window. She heard Kevin gush over finally having a son; finally, another man in the house.

Lizzie brought her nose to Mike's head. She buried her nose into his hair to smell her newborn's smell but that motherly reflex was met with the emanation of death and cordite. Blood crusted around his mouth like he'd been eating cherry pie so sloppily as if he'd been in a pie eating contest. A trickle of blood creeped down his check from the corner of his mouth like it was trying to pull his lips into a gruesome smile. Was this Hershey's blood?

She saw Mike on his first day of school proudly climbing the bus steps following his two older sisters. He led the way for his younger sister, of only two minutes. From birth, he was blazing the trail for Margaret assuring that it would be safe for her as she followed behind.

Upon arriving at school, Margaret had a meltdown when finding out that she and Mike were not in the same class. Margaret was so upset that Mike came to stay with her for the first hour until he could finally slip away and leave Margaret on her own. He knew that she just had to settle in and then she'd be fine.

Mike was the explorer; he was never afraid to charge ahead without looking. As Lizzie sat there, she realized that Mike never talked about growing up, getting big or what he wanted to be. Mike always lived for and in the moment like he knew that's all he really had. He hung on his mother like a comfy, old sweater and took care of his twin sister like more than just a doting older brother. He was the most affectionate of all her children.

Lizzie held him and brushed back his hair and kissed his forehead. Her tears landed on his skin and rolled down into his hairline. Her shoulders rocked with sobs.

"Lizzie, I'm so sorry. I'm so sorry." Kenya repeated over and over. When she said, "I had to do it." Lizzie was snapped from her stupor. She looked up at Kenya standing over the dead child and grieving mother and nodded her head in understanding. Kenya held the gun in her sweaty palm wishing she were anywhere but here and not having done what she just did.

The minivan had been abandoned by a copse between two houses. Kenya saw that two dead heads were making their way through the trees toward them drawn by the gunshot and the crying. They anxiously moved toward their next meal at a deceptive snail's pace.

"Lizzie," Kenya said and rested her hand on Lizzie's shoulder. Lizzie turned her face to Kenya, it was red, tear stained with swollen eyes waiting for Kenya to speak. "We have to go. We're not safe here."

"I can't leave him."

"I know. We can put him in the minivan. You have four more girls out there that need you. We have to go now," Kenya said calmly.

The cannibal animals were moving closer. One had fallen and was struggling to regain its feet. The other banged into a tree, nearly fell but righted itself. Nothing was going to deter either one of them.

Kenya helped Lizzie to her feet while still holding Mike. Kenya pushed the lift gate up a little higher and Lizzie gently placed Mike inside the van on top of some boxes and covered him over with a blanket. Kenya pulled Lizzie back out of the way and closed the lift gate.

Kenya took Lizzie by the arm and pulled her toward the car. Lizzie pulled back and grabbed the book with the gun inside from the box she had dropped it onto. Kenya then led her around the open passenger door and put her in the front seat as Lizzie clutched the book to her chest. Kenya walked around the car to the driver's seat and on the way there she picked up some of the salvage and threw it into the backseat.

This was the first time Kenya had ever driven a car, a moot point now. She wove a little bit instead of driving straight and was unsteady on the gas pedal, but she was getting used to the car.

Once again, they drove in silence. Kenya expected Lizzie to be crying but instead there was nothing. Lizzie looked out the window and watched the scenery slowly pass by.

"Did I ever tell you how I met Anne Marie?" Lizzie asked.

"No. Never came up. How did you meet her?"

"About six months ago, I was walking to the train after work. I was taking my usual shortcut when I saw this woman walking toward me. A guy came up behind her and tried to take off with her purse, but she wouldn't let go. Instead, she turned around and clocked the guy really good in the face and he nearly fell. Then she started swinging her purse at him again and again and with these really powerful blows. I thought she must have had a brick in her purse. When she had him on the ground, she started kicking him and ended up stabbing him in the leg with her stiletto heel. She was doing all this on stilettos! I just thought, 'that is one tough lady.' The guy was writhing on the ground, his face bleeding. She might have even broken his nose! He was grabbing his bleeding leg while she stood over him screaming at him. I stayed with her until the police arrived.

"The next day, I saw her in the coffee shop. We sat and had lunch and I asked her what the hell she had in her purse. She told me she was carrying about sixty dollars in change that her boyfriend wanted her to deposit at the bank at lunch time, but she never made it. From then on, we met for lunch at least once a week.

"If you had asked me then who I thought couldn't be rattled by anything, someone that could make it through all this with no problem? I would have said Anne Marie, no question. She was just so tough," Lizzie took a long pause, "but she just crumbled, almost from the beginning."

"I wish that she had stuck it out," Kenya said in a soft voice. "I liked her."

"Me, too," Lizzie said on an exhale. She looked back out the window again resting her head on the headrest. "All I wanted was to see my baby's face. I looked but I didn't see him. He wasn't there."

Kenya glanced up at the rearview mirror, looked back at the road and then back at her reflection. She saw a spot of blood and something that looked like a tiny fleshy glob on the front of her hat. She stopped the car and got out ripping the black and gray striped knit hat from her head throwing it on the ground.

"What are you doing?" Lizzie said sitting up straight to follow Kenya's movements.

Kenya opened the door to the backseat and found her backpack. "I'm getting another hat. That one had gotten sweaty just like you said it would."

Lizzie looked at her through the space between the bucket seats quizzically and then it became blatantly clear that the blob on Kenya's hat was very likely remnants of Mike. Lizzie looked down and frowned to herself and then turned back and faced the dashboard, looking ahead. She didn't want to think about it. She couldn't think about it. There were still four girls out there that she had to find.

Kenya slid back into the driver's seat, pulling down on the lavender crocheted hat with a crocheted pink flower that had a rhinestone in the center of it. A quick glance in the rearview mirror,

a slight adjustment, a small satisfactory smile and off they went.

Dead and Not Forgotten

"What? What's wrong?" Kenya asked, startled, slamming on the brakes of the car.

The hasty fall of modern America greatly limited the number of piloted vehicles on the roads which in turn, greatly reduced the chances of being rear-ended when stopping short. Most people still alive were hiding having pulled in the world around them like blankets on a cold night in bed.

"Michael couldn't have been turned for too long. His skin still had some warmth to it. So, the girls can't be too far from where we found him since they are probably on foot," Lizzie hypothesized.

"Yeah *if* they are on foot," Kenya stressed.

Lizzie was out of the car before Kenya had even finished responding to her.

"Lucy!" Lizzie screamed at the top of her lungs as she looked out over a field that they had stopped next to. "Lola!" She screamed even louder, cupping her hands around her mouth, turned to face the back of the car. Lizzie leaned back into the car and reached across the front seat in front of Kenya. She pressed down as hard as she could on the horn, sounding it in short beeps.

"Lizzie! Lizzie, what are you doing?" Kenya screamed as she pushed Lizzie's hand off the steering wheel. "Stop it! You're going to draw the dead heads right to us."

"Oh my God! You're right," Lizzie responded, dropping her head, resting it on the roof of the car. She sat in the door looking and thinking. She then pulled her legs into the car and shut the door. "You're right," she said again. "What am I thinking? I could be drawing them right to the kids." She folded into herself and cried. She sat bolt upright, banging her fists against her legs, seated with her face upturned, twisted in anguish. Her face was shiny with tears.

Kenya looked at Lizzie with simple helplessness. She had never faced such grief in someone else. Kenya's mind drifted back to the fight on the kitchen floor at Lizzie's parents' house. Her face slowly screwed into a grimace and tears fell down her cheeks. She coughed, sputtered sorrow, shame and regret. Lizzie was silent for one second as she looked at Kenya. She reached out and brought the girl close to her, gripping her girl tightly.

"That man," Kenya screeched. "He," she started but never finished.

"I know. I know, honeybunch. I know. Let it out. It's okay. I'm here," Lizzie soothed. Not that she wanted to see Kenya like this, but she was a little grateful to have the subject changed for a moment.

Kenya let out a new round of racking sobs. Lizzie pulled her tighter and cried with her.

"Mike. I'm so sorry. I had to. I didn't want to," Kenya said squeezing one word out slowly at a time.

"Hey, hey, hey!" Lizzie pulled back to look at the girl. Kenya would not meet her gaze. Lizzie pulled her chin up so that Kenya had to face her. Kenya's nose was running and her eyes were already swollen. "Not for one second. Do you hear me? He was done before we got there. I know that."

Kenya gripped Lizzie harder burying her face in the crook of her neck, her cheek against the rough fabric of Lizzie's bulky barn coat.

"You did what I couldn't," Lizzie whispered into Kenya's ear. "You just did what I could never do, and I thank you for that." Lizzie pulled Kenya's face back to look at her. "I'm grateful to you. Do you understand?"

Kenya nodded her head that she did.

Lizzie and Kenya held onto each other, faces buried in the other's shoulder, sobbing. They heard random raindrops bounce off the metal of the car. They didn't hear anything else such as the approaching cannibal animals. The rain fell harder; bigger drops slamming onto the roof of the car like rounds of thunder. It soothed them somewhat.

It was the slap of a hand against the passenger window that caused Kenya to raise her swollen eyes from Lizzie's shoulder. A bolt of lightning backlit the fiendishly evil face of a child peering at them, mouth agape and twitching.

Kenya screamed and counted, "One one-thousand, two-," before she was interrupted by another thunderous clap of thunder.

"Shit!" Lizzie whispered as she eyed several of the biological robotic figures ambling toward the car, some of them nearly tripping over themselves trying to get to the car and the sushi meal inside.

Hands and bodies of the dead mashed up against the windows pawing and grabbing for anything meaty to eat but only found metal and fiberglass.

"Whaddawedo, whaddawedo?" Kenya said with panic firing her words.

"Stay calm. Doors locked?" Lizzie asked and then hit the lock button. "I wonder if they can even open a door?"

The death mob covered the car like a blanket. They pushed, shoved, reached and slapped at the metal trap trying to scrape their way to the two women locked inside.

"Shit. Shit. Shit. Shit. SHIT!" Lizzie screamed. "Let me get in the driver's seat."

Kenya slid her body into the back seat so that Lizzie could move over behind the wheel. Once Lizzie was settled, Kenya moved back to the front passenger seat.

Lizzie put her hands on the wheel and stared at the bodies draped over the front of the car. "I can't see through them," she said and thought for a moment. "You know what? It's not like I should be afraid to kill any of them, right?" She chuckled.

The rain was not letting up. The drops pelted the dead bodies and any exposed space on the car's surface. Lightning and thunder exploded in the sky almost simultaneously at this point. The women were momentarily deafened by the sound and blinded by the flash. The dead noticed none of the natural phenomenon happening around them. They were completely oblivious to everything but what was in the candied metal shell.

"I don't know if I should tell you to put your seatbelt on or not, so here goes!" Lizzie said and pressed her foot lightly onto the pedal and yelled, "Just hold on!" Lizzie shifted the car into drive. It jerked slightly forward at first and then began rolling slowly. She worried that if she floored it that the car would skid with disastrous results.

Lizzie continued to move the car forward slowly. The cannibal animals toward the back of the car either held on and tried to keep up or they dropped away being left behind. Some fell. It was the dead at the front of the car posing the real problems. One ghoul had slid up onto the hood of the car and was staring at them through the windshield.

At least one or two others, likely more, had found themselves beneath the undercarriage and the wheels. It was these bodies that were slowing the car down to a stop. Lizzie was punching the gas, but the wheels only spun in response. The dead heads that had fallen away were now surrounding the car again. Kenya was begging her to get them out of there. Lizzie sat dumbly for a moment, thought of snow and sprang into action.

Lizzie had been stuck a time or two after a slippery and messy snowfall. One time in particular stood out to her. She was heavily pregnant with Lucy and Lola. She was getting ready to pop. Lizzie had an old Nissan Sentra. She and Kevin were still living in his bachelor apartment in the middle of nowhere. A fairly compact dirt road led up to the rutty driveway and it was those ruts that vexed her the nearly 10 months that she lived there.

She'd gotten stuck in one of the deeper winter ruts full of snow and ice. Heavy snow fell. Flakes landed softly in Kevin's hair as he walked around the car trying to decide how to solve the problem. She could be of little help in her current condition.

"When I say 'Go!' I want you to tap the gas and get the car rocking. I'll push from behind. Okay?" He yelled as he walked to the back of the car. She nodded and got the car rocking as he pushed. It took a bit of pushing and rocking, but the wheels finally caught. The tail of the car swayed and was freed from the icy, muddy rut.

"Hold on, honeybunch. I'll get us out of this," Lizzie said to Kenya. She started pumping the gas pedal. Punch, release, punch release. Slowly, the rocking started. It would have been better if one of them was in back of the car pushing, but that wasn't going to happen with the monster mash gathered around the them.

Lizzie kept punching the gas pedal until the rocking got stronger and more rhythmic. Although she was making some progress, the car was not yet freed from the mushy flesh beneath the wheels.

Suddenly, a miracle happened. The mob that so much wanted to rip them limb from limb while they feasted on their living flesh, fell upon or pushed against the back of the car enough to give them the push that they needed so badly. It was nothing short of a miracle. The car fish-tailed and then the tires made a direct connection to the pavement. The rubber gripped the tar. That gave the car the momentum it needed to be pushed off and send them on their way.

"Whoo-ey!" Lizzie screamed as she got the car under control and kept it moving forward. The creepy face fell away from the window and off the hood of the car. It slid to the road, and then rolled to a stop.

"You did it!" Kenya screamed in response. "There you go, you fuckers! Oops, sorry about my language."

Lizzie laughed and so did Kenya, sheepishly at first and then it turned into a deep belly laugh. It hurt and it felt good at the same time.

"It feels wrong to lecture you about being a well brought up young lady in these circumstances, as I'm sure your mother would be doing, but…" Lizzie said with a smirk.

"I know. Somehow, it just makes me feel better," Kenya said.

"I get that."

Lizzie had finally gotten the car moving freely but still was only doing about twenty miles per hour which was fast enough for the horde of cannibal animals to be left behind. It was still pouring buckets of rain with the occasional flash of lightning. The thunder was sounding later and later after the flash.

"I pray the kids are somewhere out of all of this," Lizzie commented. "I don't know what to do. I think they may be close. I'm not ready to give up today. I can't."

"It'll be dark soon. If they did duck in someplace, they might not come out again and we'll miss them if we go too far."

"We've got our flashlights, right?" Lizzie asked. "Hand me my bag, sweetie?"

Kenya pulled Lizzie's backpack from the backseat and plopped it between them on the console. Lizzie stopped the car, adjusted the bag to face her. She could already tell from the heft of the bag that her Maglite was in there.

"Got yours?" Lizzie asked and Kenya nodded affirmatively. "Knife or something? That gaggle of dead heads might not be too far away. No need of telling them where we are by shootin' off our guns."

She started the car again and turned on the headlights against darkening sky. She turned right, into a clustered neighborhood where all the houses looked very similar. The place looked like a war zone or that a tornado had hit it or maybe even both. Trash, vehicles, furniture and anything else that could be imagined littered the street and yards. Several bodies also dotted the landscape. It was like thoughtful touches added by an artist's brush to add a sense of realism.

They sat staring at the mess not saying anything. There was just the sound of the rain bouncing off the car like it was this scene's soundtrack. The intensity of the rain had lessened some but nonetheless, water was still falling from the sky.

Lizzie put the car in park and took her foot off the brake. She surveyed the street one more time, scanning for any movement. The headlights in straight beams lit up the raindrops as they passed through to the ground.

"I need to get out and check for the kids. You stay here. Stay safe. Stay dry."

"Nope. I'm going with you," Kenya responded.

With the Maglite in her left hand, and the heavy wooden handled, eight-inch-long bladed knife she'd taken from her mother's butcher block in her right, Lizzie moved down the street. Drizzle fell from a dusky, clouded sky. Kenya followed slightly behind her.

"I want to call out their names, but I know I can't. It's killing me," Lizzie spoke softly.

"I know," Kenya answered likewise. "How do you want to do this? Should we circle around each house?"

"Let's check around each house, porch, vehicle and outbuilding. Maybe we'll get lucky and they'll see us if they are here."

The women went to the first house on their right, cutting up through the longer than normal grass, right after a stand of trees. They advanced toward a shed that had its contents laid out in front of it as if it had vomited after a Saturday night drinking party. Rakes, hedge trimmers and such, along with boxes ripped open sat pillaged in front of the shed. A bag of ant killer was dumped in a pile and a push mower blocked the barn-look door.

Lizzie walked over to the shed door, pushed the mower out of the way and slowly pulled the door open. She loudly whispered, asking if anyone was in there while doing her best to shine her flashlight into the corners. She leaned in slightly to check, looking for any sign of the girls along with anything that might be useful but there was nothing.

Kenya shined her flashlight on the dark abandoned house behind them. Boards were hammered over the first-floor windows. The upper floor's windows had blinds shut tight against the world.

"Nothin' good here," Lizzie said as she walked by Kenya leading her between this house and the next.

The reach of the car's headlights faded through the fog and mist as they picked their way through the lawn of the next house.

"Careful," Lizzie warned as she shined her flashlight on the carcass of a dog that had been ripped apart. "Just because we haven't seen or heard anything yet doesn't mean that they aren't out there. Stay alert."

"Gotcha," Kenya responded nodding her head coolly. She was terrified but didn't want Lizzie to know. She flashed her light over a plastic kiddie pool adorned with giant flowers as she walked by it. It reminded her of the one she had in the backyard of an apartment house that she and her mother had lived in. She splashed while her mother soaked her feet on a hot day. No matter how hot the day got, that water was always ice cold. You could fry eggs on the sidewalk, and on one such hot day she did, and the water would still be ice cold.

"Come look at this!" Lizzie said excitedly. She knelt next to a canvas duffle bag in the front yard of a house. She pawed through the contents. "There's boxes and boxes of ammo in here."

"Awesome!" Kenya responded. She turned to go back to join Lizzie, almost two houses away. As she was about to clear the kiddie pool, a fisted hand darkened with age spots and crusted blood shot out from under the overturned pool. The hand unfolded and wrapped around Kenya's ankle like a vice.

Kenya screamed as she struggled to maintain her balance. If she fell, she knew she would lose. She would be pulled under that overturned kiddie pool and eaten, never to be seen again. She did not want that. She hammered at the hand gripping her with the flashlight. Sometimes hitting the hand and sometimes hitting her ankle.

Slowly, the pool fell back from the cannibal animal to which the hand belonged. A toothless, grinning face with a smile impossibly too wide. Its cheeks streaked with blood; the face looked up at Kenya. Kenya screamed louder than she ever thought possible. It shimmied along the ground trying to get closer to Kenya while at the same time trying to bring Kenya closer to it. Kenya slid on the wet grass and fell face first. She went into extreme panic mode. She kicked and screamed, trying to get herself lose from this decomposing fleshbag that was intent on eating her. She screamed for Lizzie to hurry and help her.

Lizzie raced over and began frantically stabbing at the woman's head. The knife either bounced off or glazed the skull.

Glass broke in a window from the house where the pool resided.

"I heard a scream!" Kenya yelled.

"It was probably just that glass breaking," Lizzie yelled still stabbing the woman with no luck and then turning toward the sound of the broken window to ascertain what the next crisis would be.

It was another slithery dead head that had broken the window. The top half of its body hung out through the window, blood exiting it's sliced open belly and pouring down the side of the house. It struggled to get out but somehow was trapped. It swung its arms reaching for the two women oblivious to the injuries it sustained. It was unable to do anything other than knock away some of the shards of glass that held it in place. It growled and snarled angrily never taking its eyes off them.

Lizzie finally realized her folly. She firmly pushed the woman's head to the side into the muddy lawn so that the temple and ear were exposed. The woman never stopped struggling. Lizzie screamed for Kenya to hold on a second more. She raised her arm, gripping the handle of the knife as tightly as she could. She brought the knife down as swiftly as possible aiming for the soft temple flesh. As the knife pierced the surface, a splat of darkened blood sprayed out all over the front of Lizzie. After, just a small rivulet began flowing down the side of the woman's head, and the formerly elderly woman went limp.

As Lizzie stood up, three dead heads, all children, were making their way toward them. Perhaps, they wanted their pool back or maybe revenge for the death of their grandmother. Whatever it was that they wanted, it was time to go.

"Grab your stuff. We gotta get out of here now!" Lizzie yelled not bothering to try to whisper. The great thing about the rain was that it was rinsing the dead old lady's blood off her face.

The broken window idiot still struggled in the pane. Two other adult-sized cannibal animals were now ambling down the street from the direction of the car.

"Head to the car and give those dead heads a wide birth. I'm getting that bag of ammo," Lizzie yelled over her shoulder as Kenya scrambled to her feet. Lizzie ran to the bag, crouched down to zip it up quickly, threw it over her shoulder and ran toward the car like she was in a relay race.

Kenya got behind the wheel, shifted the car into drive and drove toward Lizzie. Lizzie had to swerve around one of the cannibal animals as it reached out to grab her. The most it got was a graze of the canvas of the duffel bag. She whipped the car door open and threw the bag and herself into the car.

Kenya slammed her right foot down on the gas pedal. The tires spun on the wet pavement looking for purchase. They finally locked on the tar and the car catapulted forward.

"Oh my God! Did you see that Lizzie? I just burned rubber!" Kenya exclaimed. "I don't even have my license yet and I just burned rubber!" She gleefully screamed with a huge smile on her face. "Did you see that?"

"I sure did. Until this moment, I never thought that was cool, but you did it!" Lizzie responded, feeling a weird sense of pride over the girl burning rubber. The pride over the girl burning rubber surprised her but the feeling of love for her did not.

The girls hurried along down a deserted street. The rain fell so heavily that they were soaked completely through within minutes. Their sneakers squished as they walked.

The road they walked was thickly wooded on both sides. The trees reached up above their heads, their branches completely shrouded in lush spring leaves trying to catch the sun's rays, but today only caught rain drops.

All but Lucy were still crying about Mike. It wasn't that Lucy wasn't affected by Mike's death; she was. Lucy was focused on getting her sisters out of the down pour, off the road and into someplace dry and safe. Mourning Mike would have to wait.

Margaret left her sisters, walked to a tree on the side of the road and leaned against it, her head resting on her raised arm. She sobbed. She heaved. Her body shook.

Olivia came to stand beside her sister, nudging her face in between the tree and Margaret. Then Lola. Then Lucy. The foliage barely shielded them from the rain, but the closeness of kin gave some comfort.

All that could be heard were raindrops banging on a leaf and rolling on to the next. Violence struck the pavement every time bucket-sized raindrops landed. Margaret's howls were muffled into the shoulder of her oldest sister. Lola and Olivia sniffled. Snot ran down from Olivia's nose. Otherwise, there was silence in the world; nothing else moved.

A scream rose into the sky, over the treetops somewhere int the distance. Soon after a single gunshot sounded. Lucy looked up but could not see the source of the sound. She rested her head back onto Margaret's.

They did not hear it. No one did. First smell, then sight alerted them to the visage of death that was nearly upon them.

"Go!" Lucy yelled as she threw Margaret away from her. "Go, O, go!" Lucy slid Mike's backpack off her should and rooted quickly inside pulling out his utility knife. "Go guys! Lola, help me!" Lucy screamed as she moved to get between the cannibal animal and her sisters.

Lucy crouched like she was waiting for a serve in a tennis match, except instead of a racquet she had a knife ready to swing. It moved steadily toward her; it was in no rush. Lucy swung prematurely, more to scare it off than to hit it. Could these things actually be scared?

It. It? It was a teen-aged boy. He looked relatively unharmed. His shirt had some blood on it but that was it. His head was tilted slightly down so that it seemed like he was just staring at her chest; something that she had started to notice was happening more often now that her body had started to change.

He lurched forward in a large, awkward step. Lola came up behind him, having raised a thick log over her head. She brought the log down with all the strength she had. Instead of knocking him down, she propelled him into Lucy.

He fell on Lucy like the dead weight that he was, taking her down with him, pinned beneath him, mouth a-chomping inches from her face. Lucy was scrambling and twisting to get out from underneath him. She still had the utility knife in her hand and was swinging it the best that she could, but only landed grazing blows. Lola stood over the pair hitting him with the log, also to no avail.

"Pull him off of me, L!" Lucy screamed while she tried to push him off her body. He was too heavy for her. His face hung over hers. Its mouth snapped. He tried to get his teeth into her flesh. He grabbed at her and at the ground. To Lola, he looked like he was swimming. Lucy looked at him for a second and could see that at some point, not too long ago, he had been kind of cute. Now he was just terrifying and gross. "Lola!"

Instead of walking away, Margaret and Olivia stood a short distance from them staring in stunned horror, whimpering and screaming out their sister's names. They could be on their own soon.

Lucy brought her knee up to her chest, putting it between herself and the teen-age mutant cannibal. As she pushed out, Lola grabbed his shoulders and pulled. It flipped over on his back bringing Lucy with him.

The former high school heart throb was pulling on Lucy's shirt. Lucy scrambled as far away from him as she could. Once she had control of herself, she turned, raised the utility knife and plunged it into his eye. Aqueous humor squirted out missing Lucy's face. Blood and eyeball oozed down his cheek. He was finally dead. Really dead.

Lucy got up, grabbed Lola and ran to the other girls. She picked up Mike's backpack, hugged the girls and then moved them along quickly.

They came to the mouth of Seaver Street. From what they could see, it opened into a neighborhood of houses. The rain had tapered some. They looked down the dismal, ripped up street. They looked for something that would scream safety and shelter. Maybe they would find something.

"What do you think?" Lola asked looking at Lucy.

"I don't know. Maybe we can find a porch or something and go from there," Lucy replied with uncertainty.

"Should we take our knives out?" Olivia asked.

"Yeah," Lola replied on an exhale.

They dug into their bags and with knives in hand they started down Seaver Street. It was doubtful that the younger girls would even be able to use the knives they held. They proceeded cautiously, worried that a boogieman would jump out of thin air at any moment.

The houses stood dark. No movement. No life. No sound except for raindrops lightly pelting surfaces. The girls picked their way through discarded tools, toys and lives.

"There. What about there?" Margaret asked tapping Lucy's arm, pointing to a modest house with a large front porch. A kiddie pool sat overturned on the front lawn.

"Good eye, M. Let's go," Lola said.

Eyes darting in every direction, they walked across the lawn to the house. Just before they climbed the steps Lucy put her hand out to stop her sisters from going ahead. She put her fingers to her lips and climbed the three steps to the top and crossed to the door and window on tip toe.

She peeked through the window, cupping her eyes in hopes that it would help her see better. All she saw was a still, dark house. She put her ear against the pane and heard nothing. She motioned for her sisters to come up.

"I'm soaked. I want to put on something dry," Lola said as she squatted and ripped into her backpack. She didn't have much else in there other than another shirt but at least it was dry.

"I'm wet. I wanna change, too. Where can I go to change?" Margaret asked standing up with clothes in her hand.

"Right here," Lola responded and pulled off her wet shirt and put the dry one on.

"I can't! Someone will see me," Margaret whined.

"Who is going to see you?" Lucy asked.

"In the time it took you to whine about it, you could have dry clothes on. You didn't see me blink and I actually have something to see!" Lola said sarcastically.

"Yeah, that designer haircut," Lucy added.

"And boobs. She has boobs!" Olivia chimed in.

"No one will see you! Everybody is dead! There is no one left to see or help us. Don't you get it? We are all alone. It's just us, you idiot!" Lola screamed.

"I don't care. I'm not doing it. Last time," she paused. "Last time, Mike-"and she stopped.

"You're right," Lola said touching Margaret's shoulder.

Margaret burst out in tears. "It's not true. It's not true. Mommy's looking for us. She said that she would."

"No, she's not! She's dead like everyone else," Lola started again.

"Is that true?" Olivia asked on the verge of tears.

"Stop it, Lola. Stop it!" Lucy admonished her sister. She had Margaret in her arms. Lucy stroked her sister's hair to calm her.

"Gaarrah!" A cannibal animal was making its way across the littered lawn.

"No! What are we gonna do?" Olivia screamed.

"It's one of them!" Margaret said excitedly.

"Cool your jets for sec," Lucy said. She went to the door and tried the knob. It wasn't moving. "Shit!" She looked to the side of the house and saw that the porch wrapped around. "C'mon! Maybe we can jump off over on the side," Lucy yelled and led the way.

As Lucy rounded the corner of the porch, she saw a door. She peered in through the glass panes and saw an empty kitchen. She tried the handle, but it was locked. Looking around her she saw Margaret and Olivia but not Lola.

"Where's Lola?" Lucy screamed running back to where they'd come from. Lola was repacking her bag while the cannibal animal was trying to right itself after tripping over something on the lawn. "Lola! Leave it! We'll come back for it."

"I can't!"

"C'mon! We can get in the house," Lucy said grabbing Lola's shirt and Lola followed her.

At the door, Lucy hit the pane of glass closest to the doorknob with the butt of her folded-up utility knife.

"Hurry L, it's getting closer to the steps," Lola said with surprising calmness.

Lucy knocked the remaining shards of glass out of the pane. She carefully reached through and found the knob and unlocked the door. "Come on," she said, and they loaded into the house.

Once they were all in, Lucy pushed them into the breakfast nook and told them to get down on the floor and be quiet. "If it doesn't see or hear us it might go away," she said, and pulled the shade down over the window on the door and joined them.

Tensely, they quietly sat listening to the monster bump and scrape around outside, snarling and growling. The girls' silence convinced it that there was no longer a show here. Lunch was no longer being served and it moved back around to the front of the porch. Everything quieted down.

All but Lucy instantly fell asleep on the floor, dead to the world. Lucy lightly dozed in and out of consciousness but never fell very deep below the surface of sleep. She would open her eyes at the slightest creaking sound or noise. She finally gave in and joined her sisters in slumber.

Hours passed. Who knew how many? Rain was still falling lightly. It had started to get dark.

Lucy woke to a car motor. She was propped up with her back against the cool metal of the refrigerator. Hearing the noise paralyzed her. She sat wide-eyed in semi-darkness, listening. Like a cat, she moved to the window over the sink and looked out from the shadows.

She could just barely see the nose of the car. It was stopped down the street maddeningly out of sight. It looked like the interior light might be on since she could see some reflection of light on the tip of the hood.

"What are you looking at?" Olivia asked straining on her toes to see out of the window.

"There's a car down there. Just pulled up," Lucy whispered back.

The other two girls were now up and craning to look out the window as well. Light bickering about crowding, stepping on feet and placement broke out.

"Sssh!" Lola hissed.

Two car doors closed one right after the other. Lucy angled to try to see who had gotten out of the car, but they hadn't walked far enough into her field of vision.

Slowly, one person inched into view.

"Must be a lady with that kind of hat," Lola decided from the color of the knit hat that she saw.

Another person came up behind the first, tapped her on the arm. They disappeared to the left behind a fence.

"They're gone," Lucy said.

"Who was it?" Margaret asked a little too loudly.

"Sssh! Keep it down," Lola whispered loudly.

Silence and stillness held sway for some time while they stood at the kitchen window. There was no sign of the people. The girls whispered anxiously about going into the rest of the house to look out of other windows.

A female voice sounded outside nearby but the woman was out of sight. A second voice responded. The woman with the light purple hat walked by shining a flashlight on the kiddie pool as she walked past it. The first voice called out again and the light purple hat turned to go back and join her. Before she'd cleared the kiddie pool, she tripped and fell. They saw the second woman run to help. Darkness obscured them.

The girls heard stumbling coming from the room just beyond the kitchen. Lola ran to the kitchen door and looked into a dining room only to see an ancient former man stumbling toward her. She closed the door and braced herself against it to keep it closed. Lucy rushed to the door and turned the lock to secure it.

They heard glass break on the other side of the door. Agitated growling followed. The younger girls started to panic a bit, but Lucy shushed them and they quieted.

Out of the silence, banging on the kitchen door with the broken pane started. A hand came through the open broken window and pushed at the shade. Margaret screamed and Lola slapped a hand over her mouth. Lucy shushed them all again and they backed away from the door and back toward the breakfast nook.

"I thought that thing left," Margaret whispered to Lola.

"What are we gonna do?" Lola screeched.

"Shut up for a second!" Lucy responded whispering loudly.

"Don't tell me to shut up!" Lola shot back righteously.

"Like we have time for this. Stop. Work with me here. It's not like we have time to fight," Lucy whispered.

Margaret was crying. She looked out the kitchen window and said, "There's more out there. We're trapped here."

They could hear the monster in the next room moaning and moving around. They were bookended in a room with two doors that couldn't be used.

"Can we go out through the window and get onto the porch?" Olivia asked.

"Even if we do, we'll have to deal with the ones out there," Lola replied.

The girls stood at the sink and tried to figure things out. Suddenly, they heard tires squeal and the car that they hadn't been able to see went speeding past the house and out of sight again.

"Hey M," a familiar voiced called to Margaret. It blocked out the voices of her sisters brainstorming.

Margaret looked to the door leading to the rest of the house. Her tears came to a stop and her eyes widened.

"Come through here. You can get out the back," Mike said.

"We can't, M. There's one of those things in there."

"Him? He won't bother you. "C'mon!" He said with his hand on the door. "Hurry!"

Margaret walked slowly to the door, unlocked it and turned the knob.

"Margaret! What are you doing?" Lola asked anxiously.

"Don't worry. It's okay. We can get out," Margaret said as she stepped through the threshold and into the open dining room leading to the living room that took up the back half of the house.

"Margaret, wait!" Lucy yelled. Lucy followed her to see that the old man cannibal animal that was in the dining room was trapped in the window that he had broken. She followed Margaret and motioned for the others to come.

Plywood was nailed up against the back wall. It looked like it might be covering a back exit. Part of the plywood covered part of the window next to it. Through the window, they could see a patio with overturned backyard furniture silhouetted in the night.

"We can't get out this way. Everything is boarded up," Lucy said with disappointment.

"This way," Mike said standing on the bottom step of a staircase.

"Just follow me," Margaret said calmly and confidently.

The monster stuck in the window struggled and growled. He knew that there was something tasty behind him, teasing him with their tasty flesh but he was trapped, impaled on shards of glass still puttied tightly into the pane.

Margaret led them up to the second floor. She saw Mike disappear into one of the bedrooms and she followed.

"Oh, this is brilliant Margaret!" Lola exclaimed sarcastically. "How is this going to get us out?"

"Tell her to shut up, M," Mike said standing at the window. "This box right there has a ladder that hooks onto the windowsill and you guys can climb down it."

"Mike says to shut up, Lola," Margaret repeated crossing the room to the box on the floor. She pulled out a simple rope and wooden slatted ladder. "We can use this to get out through the window," she said smiling smugly.

"Mike what?" Lola asked.

Lucy crossed the room to the window. She unlocked the sash and opened it. She looked out to see a clear backyard.

"Alright guys let's see if we can find sleeping bags and maybe a change of clothes or anything useful that we can take with us," Lucy instructed.

After carefully searching the upper floor and finding no other cannibal animals and only three sleeping bags in a big hall closet, they made their way down the ladder to the backyard. Lucy first, then Olivia, Margaret and lastly, Lola.

"That ladder was fun. I would do that again," Olivia said smiling.

"I'm sure we have more fun things ahead of us," Lola said sarcastically.

Lucas and Sandrine had been driving and walking and scavenging for the last week. They would drive a car until it ran out of gas or reached a point where they could drive no further. They would abandon the car along with most of the treasures that they had accumulated and move on.

They were somewhere in the Virginia countryside, "out in the boonies," Lucas had said. They'd only seen one sign that told them exactly which town they'd landed in and it said Boonestown.

Other than that, they'd only seen the occasional road sign telling them how far they were from any given city or town.

This day found them sitting on the backyard patio of a house that sat vacant. Well, vacant unless you counted the bloodied noseless face with curlers dangling in her hair that gawked at them through a second-floor broken window with half the blinds on the outside of the house. They could hear it squeaking faintly.

"Lucas, where are we going?" Sandrine asked. Her weary eyes beseeched him for a make-it-all-better answer. She wore a diamond choker that hung loosely around her neck. It was jewelry meant for a grown woman.

Lucas pushed a saltine cracker sandwich that was overstuffed with dry tuna deep into his mouth and chewed, mouth open. It was like watching clothes rolling in a dryer at the launderette. He sat back in the patio chair and looked at Sandrine thoughtfully. "You're tired, huh?"

Saying nothing, her dark-circled, rounded eyes stared back at him.

"You're right. We need to find a place and lay low a bit. Maybe hook up with others?"

"Maybe," she responded almost inaudibly. She was too tired to speak.

"I'm sorry my little side hooligan. I forget that you're only six because you're such an invincible side hooligan. Before the world hit the fan your life was all bedtime stories, dolls, and tea parties for you, huh?"

She nodded her head in the affirmative.

"Okay, yeah," he sighed and sat thinking. "Okay. Okay. Here's the plan. This house is out. Let's find another in this neighborhood with a fence. There's gotta be one out there with a fence. We'll clean it out if it's not too bad and then keep 'em out after that. How's that sound?"

"Good," she croaked with a small smile and swung her feet. She was still short enough that her feet didn't touch the ground when she sat in a chair.

The search had taken the better part of a day and the sun was quickly lowering itself in the sky. There were three houses in the near vicinity that had fenced in yards. Two of the houses only had the backyard fenced in still leaving the front of the house exposed to the undead threat. The third house was completely fenced with a chain link running across the front and over the driveway. The backyard had high stockade fencing providing the privacy and safety they needed.

They stood in the street looking at the surroundings of the third house and listened. The house wasn't as well kept and pretty as the houses that surrounded it, but pretty wasn't what they were looking for. Birds twittered in a nearby tree. Otherwise, the area was quiet.

The front door creaked opened. A woman slowly moved herself into the doorway, pushing her walker out first. She put her hand over her eyes like a visor despite the day being no longer very bright. She stood there assessing them.

"Just gonna stand there?" She yelled. "Get in here before you attract 'em all over here."

Lucas and Sandrine looked at each other. Lucas cocked his head to the side and Sandrine nodded okay.

They opened the gate across the driveway no more than necessary and slipped through to the yard. The woman reminded them to shut the gate despite seeing them in the process of doing so. Approaching the door slowly with Sandrine moving close behind him, Lucas introduced themselves to the woman.

"I'm Hazel. It's just me and the boy here so I hope you don't bring trouble with you."

"Glad to meet you," Lucas said offering his hand.

"Well, aren't you a pretty little thing? Better get in here before any of those things see ya."

As she ushered them in moving much faster than when they'd first seen her, Lucas took her in. From a distance, Hazel looked much older, almost elderly. Up close, she couldn't have been more than forty. There was some gray woven into her stringy dark hair, but her face was youthful, nearly without lines.

They came to stand in the middle of a very dimly lit parlor. There were several candles lit on an end table. More light from the outside could have filtered in if the windows weren't shut tightly with curtains. Puzzle books and a full astray lay on the coffee table.

The air was thick. Both Lucas and Sandrine were finding it difficult to breathe. There was a sense of pressure pushing down on them, so much so, that the best they could do was take short shallow breaths. The air smelled more of something than just cigarette smoke. Neither tell what that 'more' was. Whatever it was, it did not smell good.

"Sit down," Hazel said as she held on to her walker and backed herself into her recliner. Behind her appeared to be part of a grape jelly sandwich smeared on the wall. In this light, it almost looked like thick, cakey blood.

Lucas and Sandrine walked around the coffee table to sit on a pile of blankets covering the sofa.

"Saw you through the window. You looked harmless enough. Didn't want to leave you out there. With things the way they are, we gotta try to stick together, right? You kids from around here?"

"About a town away. We're just out looking for supplies," Lucas said.

"Casing my house, huh?" Hazel asked with a caught ya kind of smirk.

"No. We thought we heard dogs barking and we were trying to figure out where it was coming from," Lucas spit out the lie quickly. He didn't feel safe telling her anything about what they were really doing.

A face peeked out from around a corner, mostly obscured by the shadows. Dark hair fell over a dark eye of a man in his early twenties. Sandrine gasped in surprise not realizing fully that anyone else had been in the house. Hazel had mentioned a boy, but to this point there had been nothing to indicate that there actually was one. This man was clearly not a boy. Maybe there was a boy somewhere else in the house.

"Get back in your room. You know that you're not fit for company!" Hazel barked at the young man. "Bastard," she said under her breath.

"Is that your son?" Sandrine asked quietly.

"Him? The boy? God, no! He's no son of mine," Hazel answered looking back at the corner to take another look at him, but he was gone. She never gave an explanation as to who the man was.

"Then who is he?" Sandrine pressed. "Can he come out? I want to meet him."

"No. The boy ain't coming out. I told you he ain't fit for company." Hazel said scratching a raised, black mole high on her cheek next to her nose.

Now that his eyes had adjusted to the lack of light in the room, Lucas was looking around and figuring out that this was a place that they did not want to be. The back end of a cat was sticking out from under another recliner. If it was just that, it wouldn't be alarming but what looked like entrails and a dark blood stain also seeped out from under the recliner.

On the kitchen counter was a bowl covered with a stained dishtowel. There was a swarm of flies buzzing round it. Lucas looked over to the corner to see the young man leering at Sandrine with what seemed like malevolent intent. Once the man licked his lips Lucas was certain the intent was malevolent.

"Well," Lucas said as he stood. "We need to get started back."

"Walking?" Hazel asked.

"We have a car down the street a bit."

"You have gas? There's still gas?"

"It's a car we found," Lucas answered.

"A car thief, is it?" Hazel said smirking again with one eye cocked, giving off a suspicious and accusatory look.

"Is there even such a thing anymore?" Lucas responded walking Sandrine quickly to the door.

"Thank you for inviting us in," Lucas said as he gripped the knob, turned it and thanked God that it wasn't locked. He opened the door, pushed Sandrine out and then slammed it shut behind them. They both took deep breaths of badly needed fresh air while they rushed back down the drive. Hazel had come to the door and was yelling after them to come back and check in with her from time to time.

As Lucas turned to lock the gate, he saw the boy on the side of the house looking at Sandrine and rubbing his groin area. He winked at Lucas with a creepy sneer. Lucas shivered.

"I couldn't breathe in there. As bad as it can smell out here, it was worse in there," Lucas said as they walked down the street.

"There was something really wrong in that house."

Lucas' eyes opened to the just rising sun as it peeked through the trees. Sandrine's eyes were still shut tight against the world. She lay curled up in a ball on the passenger side floorboards cuddled in a blanket. They were in the cab of an old pickup truck that they'd found last night.

They had walked less than a mile before coming across the truck. It had been past dusk and the real night had started to set in. They were lucky to find it and luckier still that one of the doors was unlocked and no one was in it waiting to eat them. The only problem was that it was in the middle of the street, a higher profile than Lucas would have liked. There were no keys to move it to a more camouflaged spot.

He got her fed with a can of baked beans last night and she was asleep before she finished. He grabbed the half empty can and poured the contents into the last clean plastic sealable bag that he had. Wasting food was a thing of the past.

Lucas slowly sat up. He had sprawled out over the length of the bench seat. He groaned quietly as he straightened out. His back was killing him.

He slid behind the wheel and stared out through the windshield. He quietly opened the glovebox and found nothing more than the registration. When he opened the ashtray, he found the prize. The keys sat nestled within. Lucas grinned.

Lucas surveyed the landscape surrounding the truck. Heavy woods on one side and a front lawn on the other. A house was set far back at the end of a long driveway. They hadn't been able to see the house last night in the dark.

Lucas looked down at Sandrine. She was still sleeping. Her mouth was slightly open with a string of drool running down her chin. Her dark hair fell across her eyes. He really needed to get her to brush that burgeoning rat's nest. He wasn't even sure if she had a brush with her. When they found a house, he would get her cleaned up. He thought about how nice it would be to clean himself up. He tried to remember his last shower and thought it must have been that first night on the road his way home from college.

That first night, he'd pulled off the interstate exit and paid for a room at small roadside motel. It was during that night that he'd gotten his first inkling that something was up. Commotion outside woke him from a deep sleep. It never quieted down enough to fall back to sleep. The other travelers had been outside the motel talking, yelling and making noise. Once he realized that he'd gotten all the sleep that he was going to get, he decided to get going. He hit the road before the sun came up that day and saw his first zombie by noontime. It was something he never thought he'd ever see in a million years.

The street was quiet. Nothing was moving around them. He could hear a few birds chirping but not as many as he would expect on a late spring morning. Lucas looked from Sandrine to the house and back. He debated leaving her to go check out the house, but this could be just what they needed.

By opening the truck door slowly, Lucas hoped to keep the hinges from creaking and waking up Sandrine. He slipped out before he'd opened it very far. The door creaked a smidge, but not as bad as it would have had he opened it far more. He shut the door softly without engaging the lock. He looked in through the window and saw that Sandrine was still sleeping. She hadn't moved.

The sun was now higher in the sky, just above the trees behind the house. Lucas scanned every direction and saw nothing. He walked down the long driveway hoping and praying that this house would be as close to perfect as possible. Sandrine really needed a rest and if he was being honest with himself, he did too. In the near distance two bunnies hopped so quickly away it was as if they were gliding on top of the grass.

The house and the yard around it looked idyllic. The further down the drive Lucas got, the more he could see. There was an elaborate and expensive swing set/jungle gym combination just beyond the back of the house. He could also see that someone had started a sizable garden. Although it had its fair share of weeds, it wasn't so far gone that some elbow grease couldn't fix it. This place was looking better and better.

As he got closer, Lucas' pace slowed. He was listening and looking for anything that would send him running back to the truck and Sandrine. Sandrine! He stopped and looked back at the truck. Quiet.

He climbed a small set of steps and tried the storm door. It opened. He tried the knob of the inner kitchen wooden door and it turned easily. His heart leapt with excitement. Lucas slowly pushed open the door and called out, "Hello?" He listened with bated breath for any kind of response. He could hear his heart beating in his chest; it was so quiet. He left the door open behind him and stepped into the center of the kitchen. Everything was neat and orderly as if whomever lived there just stepped out for a moment and maybe that was the case.

It was easy to see that this house was occupied by a young family. The refrigerator was loaded with family pictures of little kids posed and candid, just doing little kid things. One picture caught an infant peeing into the air during a diaper change. Another was of two younger children, maybe 4 and 6, playing on the swing set out back. The family looked happy. There was evidence of the family in every corner of this house, but they were not home.

Lucas went through the cabinets and found an ample supply of non-perishable food with even more in a side pantry. These people hadn't been doomsday preppers, but they did have quite a bit of food stored with more fresh food on the way. With what was in the house, and the potential of the garden, this could keep them fed for quite some time if they were careful.

He made his way through each of the bedrooms. He caught sight of himself in a mirror in the master bedroom. His hair was a mess. He had dirt and blood smeared on and grimed into his face. Lucas looked down at his hands. He had so much dirt under his nails that they were black.

Dirty nails were the bane of his mother's existence. She would get all over him for such an undignified offense if she were here. She often told him that nothing was more disgusting than dirty nails. No gentleman would be caught dead with dirty nails. Well, he wasn't dead yet, but she certainly was.

The nursery had baby wipes. He grabbed the box and took them to the bathroom. Looking in a mirror, Lucas thought he looked like a lunatic. He couldn't find himself under all that dirt, grime, and dried blood. He set about cleaning himself up. The cool baby wipe felt so good on his skin. He closed his eyes and just enjoyed the feeling for a moment before he set to scrubbing his face and hands.

Lucas scoured the basement and had just put his foot on the first basement step to come back up into the kitchen when he heard it. Gunshots. Not just one but one after the other and sometimes two at a time or fired close together. "Sandrine!" He screamed.

Lucas sprinted up the steps pulling his gun from the waistband of his pants. As he raced out of the house, he saw it. The old pickup truck was surrounded by them. Cannibal animals of nearly every variety, tall, short, fat, skinny, adult, child. They either clawed at the cab of the truck or were clawing their way to the cab of the truck.

The monsters were being shot at by some unseen force. Lucas wasn't far enough down the driveway to see what or who it was. Some of the cannibal animals would get hit in the head and fall away. Others would be hit in the body. They would jerk, but it would not deter them from their object of affection for very long. It was no more than a mosquito bite or bee sting to them. There were more shots being fired than were dead bodies being eliminated. Lucas realized that whomever it was shooting had very poor aim, for the most part.

Lucas ran screaming Sandrine's name and for the shooters to stop shooting. He saw her head pop up once but that was it. He prayed that she was okay.

Through some thinning trees, Lucas began to see the shooters walking toward the truck. There were four of them. All of them appeared to be male from where Lucas stood. One wore a cowboy hat, a holster and gun belt with bullets in every loop encircling his impossibly slim waist and was using a six-shooter.

Another had a red bandana tied around his head holding down his dark, curly hair with crisscrossed bandoleers wrapped around his significant torso. Skinny, chicken legs led up to a belly so big that the bandoleers shrank away from it, rising up, looking bunched and awkward. They appeared to be so tightly draped about the man that Lucas was wondering how he was breathing. This man was shooting a semiautomatic rifle nonstop. He didn't seem to be taking aim. He just shot haphazardly from the hip.

Where the first two men were white this third one had the most beautifully tanned skin and short, dark hair. A bit stocky, he was dressed simply in a pair of jeans, boots, and a white t-shirt. He carried an automatic handgun and would shoot at intervals. He really tried to make hits, but seldom did.

The fourth was African American. He wore a coonskin hat replete with racoon tail and carried a rifle. Of average build, he carried himself with confidence. When he shot, he made the kill every time.

Making his presence known was dangerous, but Lucas needed to protect Sandrine and get them to stop shooting. He continued shouting for them to stop. With all the commotion, they didn't hear him until they saw him running down the driveway. It was then their guns were pointed at him, but they thankfully weren't shooting. Lucas and the group continued to cautiously walk toward each other. Lucas raised his hand holding the gun above his head to show that he was not a threat to them. They stopped within one hundred feet of one another.

There were still a few cannibal animals meandering around and clawing at the truck. Ones that had been knocked down worked extremely hard at regaining their footing.

The passenger door flew open, the four guns swung to point at the cause. Out came Sandrine running at full bore. Lucas screamed for them not to shoot. Sandrine pushed two of the zombies to the ground and ran to Lucas. Once she reached him, she hugged him as tight as she could.

Lucas held her tight as well and asked her if she was okay. He pushed her away slightly to check her all over for any injuries. She had a tear in one of her sleeves below her shoulder. Blood was running down her arm and turning the rest of the sleeve red.

The four men walked toward the couple with little caution. All but one of them had holstered or lowered their guns. The last still held his hunting rifle on them. As they gathered around Lucas and Sandrine, he remembered himself and lowered his rifle.

Lucas could see that they were not men at all, but rather four teen-aged boys that weren't likely more than sixteen years old. The boys asked all at once if Sandrine was okay and apologized for shooting at the truck. They were so sincere in their concern that Lucas quickly saw that they were of no threat to him and Sandrine.

"I'm just grateful you didn't kill her," Lucas said as he continued to check her. "Is this the only place you're hurt?" Lucas asked feverishly.

"I think so," Sandrine answered. She wasn't sobbing, but tears slid from her eyes. "It hurts. My arm hurts. It burns."

"Here! Here!" said one of the boys ripping off his heavy backpack and then then the white t-shirt he was wearing. He started ripping it into strips and then handed them to Lucas. "Use this to bandage her arm."

Lucas thanked him. He ripped away the rest of Sandrine's sleeve and looked at the wound. He wiped away the blood and saw that it was more like a deep scrape and thankfully not a full-on bullet wound. He put a wad of t-shirt directly on the scrape and then wound and tied a strip of t-shirt around it to hold it on.

"Hey man, we really are sorry. We didn't know," the one with the six-shooter and cowboy hat said.

"Yeah dude, we didn't know she was in there," the red bandana wearing boy said.

"I'm Lucas and this is Sandrine," Lucas said introducing himself and extending his hand.

"John," the t-shirt wearing boy said and shook his hand.

"I'm Bob," the red bandana boy said.

"Danny," the coonskin cap boy said and shook Lucas's hand.

"James," the last said as he took his hand from resting on the butt of his gun in the holster and shook Lucas' hand.

Sandrine looked at them shyly not saying anything. She had melted into Lucas' body as much as she could. She was no longer scared; she was just in shock.

By this point, the few cannibal animals left had regained their feet and were wandering over for breakfast.

Danny nonchalantly walked over to each one and knifed them in the eye socket with his Bowie Knife. He did it with such grace and lack of ceremony that it was as if he'd been doing this his entire life.

"Danny is a horrible shot, but he makes up for it with that knife," Bob commented.

"You wish you could hit the side of a house, Bobby boy," Danny retorted good-naturedly as he walked back to rejoin the group.

"I'm glad that none of you were better shots. I need to find a drug store now. I want to get some real bandages and antibiotics for Sandrine before that wound gets ugly."

"We got you on that. Truck work? It's not far," Danny said as he returned to the group wiping the blade of this knife off before he re-sheathed it.

"I think so. Found the keys this morning. Wish I'd seen them last night. Let's go," Lucas said.

The truck turned over easily and had the type of engine rattle that was more personality than any indication of defect. Three of the boys hopped in the bed while Danny rode in front with Lucas and Sandrine. Danny took them straight to the drug store in the small town.

The drug store was deserted   and had been somewhat ransacked. Lucas had Sandrine sitting on the pharmacy counter. He had wiped the wound clean with hydrogen peroxide and then rubbing alcohol. She was howling in pain, but Lucas wanted to be overly cautious. Something like this could easily get infected.

"Here's some amoxicillin," James said handing Lucas a bottle over the counter.

"Thanks, man. What do you say? How about we take one every four hours?" Lucas suggested to Sandrine.

"How are we gonna know when four hours is up?" Sandrine asked.

"Good question. I used my phone as a watch for a long time. Lately, it doesn't matter what time it is anymore. That works out for me because my phone is dead. I need to get with the times, I guess," Lucas surmised.

"Like the rest of the world," James quipped.

"I've got a watch. I'll keep track. Least I can do," Bob offered.

Lucas thanked him and then started preparing the bandages. He made a good wad of gauze squares and then slathered them with an antibiotic ointment and then taped it to her arm. "We can change these when you take your next pill. Okie dokie?" Lucas asked.

"Okie dokie," Sandrine responded.

The six sat around and ate what food they could find that had not gone bad. For once, fake food full of preservatives was a good thing. It put something in their bellies to keep them from growling.

James had found several boxes of Twinkies and ripped into one, eating the whole box. They were just as fresh and springy as they had been when they came off the conveyor belt.

John explained that they'd all been on a school bus on their way home having been dismissed early because of what was happening all around them. The four boys went to an agricultural school about twenty miles, give or take, from where they lived. They were always the last four on the bus the last ten miles of the trip. The bus driver stopped to help someone and that someone turned out to be one of those monsters and the rest was history. They'd been wandering and scavenging the area ever since.

James and Danny were the only ones with any experience with guns. Both had hunted with their fathers. Danny was a marksman, trained by his Marine father. James was an okay shot. He could never live up to his father's expectations. John said that he wasn't entirely comfortable with a gun in his hand, but thought he'd better get used to it.

Talk eventually turned to what they would do next and Lucas explained what his thoughts had been about the house prior to encountering the four boys. He mentioned that it might need some cleaning out with all the shooting that had taken place there earlier today but if they were game, so were he and Sandrine.

Lucas parked nearly in the same spot that the truck had been in when they first found it. He reasoned that by not parking it in the driveway it would keep others from thinking the house was occupied. They might just take the truck and go. Plus, at this point, vehicles were still all over the place. If they needed one, they could get one.

As soon as they pulled up, cannibal animals in the near vicinity started to approach the truck. There were about fifteen of them. Lucas explained his and Sandrine's method of knocking them over and then stabbing them in the head. Danny threw in his two cents of stabbing them through one of the eyes if possible since that tissue was soft. They buddied up and took all fifteen down in short order.

Over the next two weeks they got the house in order. The garden was cleaned up. The boys had done some hunting with James and Danny taking the rest in tutelage. In fact, they were all exchanging information. They started to line the property with whatever fencing they could dig up or steal from stores, other houses or made from scratch. They got to know each other. They were making their own little community.

However, talk always returned to families. The boys talked about making it back to their homes to learn the fate of their families. None had any contact with them since the day on the bus. Their cell phones stopped working the next day. Prior to that, all had reached a parent or sibling, and no one had succumbed to the devastation around them. All the boys had hope that they would still find their families intact. All were homesick and wanted to go home to find out what waited for them or feared what was not waiting for them any longer, all except for James. He had been relieved and disappointed to hear his father's voice that last day.

It was a beautiful day. The sun was out. The sky was cloudless after all the rain. They were all in the garden weeding. Sandrine was gathering some strawberries that had finally reddened. She loved strawberries. Her mother loved strawberries. The thought made her feel lonely. She looked at Lucas and the others bent to their tasks. Some chatting away quietly, others deep in thought.

Sandrine walked over to Lucas and whispered a question into his ear. He smiled and replied that he thought that would be a great idea. He was pleased that her arm was nearly healed, and with no complications. He realized further still what a strong little girl she was. She had only complained about the itching when the skin started to re-knit itself and become whole again.

"Guys, I have a question," Sandrine said loudly. The boys all looked up from their weeding. "Guys, I want to know if you all want to be invincible side hooligans with me and Lucas."

There was some giggling but there was also a resounding yes. They had become a unit, but this made them official. They came together. Hands were shaking and Sandrine got hugged. It was that simple.

He watched from a small hole he'd carved in the fence. The hole might have been small, but the view was large. He had himself wedged against tree. It had taken him nearly a week to find her and since then he'd been back nearly every day. Each day, he waited for her to wander far enough away from the boys so that he could snatch her. Or better yet, he waited for her to wander off by herself. Then he would have her. He had so many plans for her.

He carved his name in the tree. This was the thirtieth time he'd carved or marked the fence or a nearby tree this way.

Audacity of Hope

The thing was, they weren't far from where any of the boys lived if they were going by car. They loaded up in the truck and headed to James' house first. The road conditions had gotten rougher with more and more debris clogging up the passages. Large tree limbs, abandoned vehicles, dead bodies of all species and description, and the belongings castaway whether lost or intentional, of all type. Going was slow.

The obstructed streets forced them to move like the world had become a life-sized maze with at least four possible outcomes. It was a constant seeking for the path of least resistance which landed them in Danny's neighborhood by default.

The outside landscaping of the house had taken on an apocalyptic trash motif instead of the well-kept green lawn, colorful flowers and manicured shrubbery that had always been something Danny's mother cultivated. Deeply gouged tire tracks dug up the front lawn from one side to the other, leaving dark dirt long buried pulled up and exposed to the horror of a world it had never seen. His mother couldn't be too happy about that.

Furniture lay splayed haphazardly across the lawn. Danny didn't recognize any of it. There were a few broken windows with plywood nailed into place from the inside to seal the holes. Shards of glass danced around the frame at random angles like jagged teeth. The screen door at the front of the house was hanging by the lower hinge at an angle. It appeared to have been ripped away from the frame at the top.

The Side Hooligans stared at the house from the street. They pored over the house and what surrounded it looking for any movement, any sign of life or non-life. Everything was still.

"Whaddya think Danny?" James asked.

"I think things are good here," Danny replied, smiling. He walked slowly toward the house. "Walk only where I walk. I'm serious," he said looking for understanding from everyone. "My dad most likely has the place booby-trapped."

James chuckled. "That sounds like him, alright."

Danny took small, careful, measured steps. He didn't move forward until he was certain of the safety of the next footfall. He stopped and carefully lifted his foot over a seemingly invisible barrier. He placed his foot squarely on the ground, shifted his weight and then slowly brought his other foot over. "Fishing line here," Danny said swinging his index finger over a difficult to detect trip wire until he pointed it out. "Hold up. Another one. Wait a sec," he said, head down, repeating the careful movements. He surveyed the new space and then waived the others on.

They made it most of the way to the house before they encountered more fishing line. This time, there were three lines running at angles to one another when the first lines had been more parallel.

The second set of lines were more of a puzzle. The first two lines were at different heights and angles from the ground and intersected one another.

The third line presented more of a challenge at first. It was one and a half feet off the ground, running from one tree to another. It was too high to step over confidently and too low to easily crawl under it. They talked about it a bit and then decided that they would shimmy under it like it was a limbo stick. Bob went to suck in his considerable belly only to realize that it wasn't as considerable as it had once been.

Once at the door, Danny knocked twice, slid his knuckles against the wood to below the knob, and knocked again. There was silence and then the curtain slid ever so slightly to the side. A sliver of a face with one eye appeared. It was Danny's father. He smiled and the sounds of locks and bolts releasing their holds on the door sounded.

When the door finally opened a hand shot out grabbing Danny and pulling him into the house. His father had him in a tight embrace and soon his mother and sister were wrapped around him.

At last, Danny's father raised his eyes. His cheeks were wet with two tracks leading down to his jawline. His eyes scanned the rest of the kids. "Who do you have with you? James? Is that you?"

"Yes, sir. It's me, James, Mr. Bostwick. This is John and Bob from school. They were on the bus with us. That's Lucas and

Sandrine," he pointed at each as he went. "We met them along the way."

"Alright. Hurry up and get in here," Mr. Bostwick said. "Be quick now."

The kids piled quickly into the small and narrow galley kitchen. Danny was being held onto tightly by his mother and sister while Mr. Bostwick ushered each of the kids in through the door, he touched each lightly on the back as if he was counting them.

The sun had set. Darkness shrouded them save for the bank of candles amassed on the center of the dining room table that they all sat around. The curtains were pulled tight covering the plywood that was nailed over the bay.

They sat huddled, close to one another. Extra chairs had been pulled in to seat all the additional visitors. Normally, this room and this table only offered itself to this many people on holidays and special occasions. Danny sat nestled between his mother and sister, reluctant to let him get too far from them.

"Managed to get home before it really got crazy. Got the girls situated and then went out looking for you," Mr. Bostwick said. "At times, I wasn't sure what to do."

The last comment shocked Danny. For as long as he could remember, his father had always known what to do, what to say. The man never appeared at a loss.

"When it started, your mother just barely got Elisa home from school. After I got your last call," Mr. Bostwick said pointing to Danny without lifting his hand from the table, "I headed over to where I thought the bus was. I never thought about knowing that route until I couldn't find you. We put you on the bus. We trusted that you're old enough to take care of yourself. No one expected anything like this to happen. Why would I ever need to know the route until now? I went out every day looking for you. Every day."

"He did," Mrs. Bostwick confirmed. "The first emergency messages on the television said to stay home with the doors locked. 'Don't let anyone in. Stay away from infected persons,' they said."

"Some radio stations played music like nothing was happening. Other stations just talked about conspiracy theories and how to kill these new kinds of people," Mr. Bostwick said.

"How can you kill someone you know like that? These were neighbors, friends, family," Mrs. Bostwick said through tears.

This, too, shocked Danny. His mother could be emotional, but she was no crier. She was affectionate, but even-tempered like his father. A generally pleasant woman, he couldn't recall the last time that he'd seen her cry.

"Mom, you had to," Elisa said as she leaned against her mother and nestled her head into her mother's shoulder in an attempt to comfort her.

"Within a week the TV went to snow. Then the radio stopped squawking. No music. No conspiracy theories. Just static. The last messages on the radio were telling us to go to refugee centers in Fredericksburg, Culpeper, and Charlottesville. They said that they had food, shelter, protection and medicine there. Some radio stations said these places were already being overrun by those stinkin' flesh bags. So bad at one place, soldiers mowed down the flesh bags and the living, alike. Decided at that point to just stay put," Mr. Bostwick paused tracing an invisible circle on the table's surface. "I still went out looking for you. I found the bus, dead bodies and a whole lot of blood, but I didn't find you. I thanked God for that."

Danny met his father's eyes. The connection between them shut out everyone and everything surrounding them. A tear slipped from the lashes of his lower lid and raced toward the crease of his nostril.

"Anyone left in the neighborhood?" James asked intentionally changing the subject.

"Last I checked, about five houses down on the left," Mr. Bostwick responded. "We had words over one of the houses in between and that's been it. I let them have it. We have enough to last us. They don't. Haven't seen them since, but they are still there."

"Your dad was right all along. He always said we had to be ready, that the government wasn't always going to be there," Mrs. Bostwick said.

"He also said that was why his tax money was going to waste," Elisa added resulting in laughter.

"The writing was on the wall after Katrina," Mr. Bostwick said with the response being largely lost amid the moment of levity. The kids were too young to really remember or know what Katrina was.

"Have you seen any of those walking flesh bags up close, Dan?" Mrs. Bostwick asked.

"Depends on how close you mean. On the bus, yeah, and then we jumped off and ran. In a store, once. He was covered in blood mostly. Really just been trying to keep our distance."

"Killed any?" Elisa asked.

Danny looked down at his hands. A tear landed between his fingers. "Sorry," he said sucking mucus to the back of his throat. "Haven't thought about it until now. I didn't think about them being people until now, but yeah. I've killed some."

"We haven't had much time to think about much other than just trying to stay alive," Lucas spoke, his voice cracked at the end.

"Sweetheart, God knows what's in your heart," Mrs. Bostwick said. She slipped from her chair, stood behind Danny and draped herself over him.

"Dad says God always has a hand in everything. Even if it doesn't make sense to us at the time, it will later," Elisa offered in her way of comfort.

"I think it's going to be a long time before any of this makes sense," John concluded. He and Bob had been sitting at one end of the table quietly and listening. "Mr. Bostwick, have you been over by my house at all? It's over across the tracks by the Circle K."

"I was over that way last week. Most of that area burned to the ground. Don't know what started it, but I do know that there was no Fire Department to put it out. Could have been the rain we got that stopped it. I don't know where your house is, but it might be worth a look just so you know what happened."

John dropped his head to the table, slamming his forehead against the surface. There was silence and then racking sobs. His body heaved and he fell to the floor, curling into a fetal ball. Sandrine scrambled to him and tried to hug him. She reminded him that they were Side Hooligans and that no matter what that they would stick together.

"My mom was alone!" John screamed. "She just had my little brothers. She needed me!"

Sandrine recoiled from his screaming, but then held on tighter than she had before.

"Look son, she may not have been there. The Guard was going through areas at the beginning and evacuating people," Mr. Bostwick said as he helped Mrs. Bostwick to get John up off of the floor. "I heard that they were over there toward the beginning of this thing. She might be alright and in one of the refu-," Mr. Bostwick stopped himself thinking better of it.

This helped John a little bit. "Okay. Maybe her and my brothers are still out there. I can find them if they are."

"John, we'll go check it out. You'll find something," James assured him.

"Alright boys," Mr. Bostwick started and then remembered, "and young ladies, let's get some sleep. Danny, sit up and take watch with me."

Mrs. Bostwick moved around the house grabbing what blankets and pillows that she had and put the boys in the large living room fighting it out for the best furniture to sleep on. She hustled Sandrine off to Elisa's room and tucked the girls in. They could be heard talking softly and giggling for some time.

Mr. Bostwick and Danny climbed a ladder at the back of the house and sat on the roof looking out over the neighborhood, hidden by the heavy foliage of the trees overhead. Glowing light from a full moon high overhead lit up the street with an almost supernatural aura. It was the kind of light that implies magic. The moon looked like it was close enough to swallow them whole. Its light danced through the leaves playing on the skin of father and son.

They sat alert for any movement or sound. Eyes moved over the neighborhood looking for movement, no matter how slight. Ears listened for anything that would betray an intruder, no matter how faint.

Mr. Bostwick put his hand on Danny's shoulder, squeezed and let go. He exhaled loudly. "I knew you were out there. I knew you'd find your way home," he said as he pulled a pack of cigarettes out of his shirt pocket. He popped a cigarette into his mouth, slipped his matches from the package's cellophane and lit up. He sucked in a deep drag, and then slowly exhaled blowing the smoke out from in a long white line.

"Dad, you're the toughest and smartest guy I ever met. Even still, I was scared that you, mom, Elisa wouldn't be here. I didn't want to find out that you were all gone. This isn't like anything we ever talked about."

"I know, son. The is some son of a bitch, isn't it? Yeah? Times like this, I wish I never quit smoking," Mr. Bostwick said and chuckled. "Something's going to kill you; it should be something enjoyable."

"But Dad, you said you never wanted to end up with a bunch of tubes stuck in you and hacking up disgusting phlegm like your dad."

"That's still true, but that's not going to be something that I'll have to worry about now," he said. He anchored the cigarette in the corner of his mouth. He pulled up his pant leg almost to the knee. Beneath the denim, was a small chunk missing out of the back of his calf. It didn't look like a bite mark. It wasn't even circular, but it was deep, red, fleshy and festering.

"Dad," Danny said in a horrified whisper. "Dad, no. What happened?"

"I was dealing with one when another one came out from under a porch and that was all she wrote," said Mr. Bostwick in the most matter-of-fact tone he could muster.

"Dad," Danny said again quietly.

"I'm glad you're back, Danny. Your mother is going to need your help with your sister. Elisa is too young to take care of herself in this."

"I don't know if I can without you."

"I've done everything that I could to teach how to be ready for when this day came. 'Course I didn't think this day would look like this, but here we are," Mr. Bostwick said.

They stood on the street at the end of the driveway in front of James' house. The yard and the house looked an awful lot like what Danny's house looked when they found it. The difference was that James' house often looked this way. His father wasn't much on yard work and keeping up outward appearances. That kind of stuff cut into the drinking and carousing time at the bar and his frequent hunting trips with his best friend that shared the same ambitions in life.

His father hadn't always been that way. When his mother was alive, his home life was a lot like Danny's. His mother had died during childbirth resulting in James becoming an only child at ten years-old and his father a despondent widower that given up on most things that didn't involve him wrapping his right hand around a beer bottle or a trigger.

"Do you think that's him?" John asked. From the street, they could hear the growling and banging of some cannibal animal trapped inside the house.

"I don't know. Probably is," James replied flatly.

"Do you want to go check it out?" Lucas asked.

James looked at the house. His expression was so indiscernible that it was like a cloud wrapped around a mountain top. "Not really. "S'pose I have to, though."

James led the group down the short driveway. He climbed the three steps to reach the kitchen door on the side of the house. He bent slightly at the waist, shielded his eyes and looked in through the kitchen window. He could see his father banging on a wall in the living room. James laughed. His father looked silly.

"What could you possibly be laughing at?" Bob asked. He was standing at the foot of the small set of stairs.

By this point, James was hysterically laughing. He tried to explain through the bursts, but he couldn't get it out. Instead, he yelled, "Whoa!" and stepped back quickly. The railing of the small porch hit his lower back and stopped him from falling off and onto the ground below.

James' father's face appeared suddenly in the kitchen door window. James looked at him, mesmerized. Except for his eyes being glazed over, he looked like the man James had lived with the last six years. Gin blossomed face, furrowed brow and grimace, a slight tinge of blue, gray and to his skin. This life after death hadn't changed his father much at all. He still looked miserably frustrated and incredibly pissed off. That was the father James knew.

His father beat on the door. The door shook in its frame. James stared at him, no longer laughing, expression blank. His father snarled and growled and clawed at the door, banging his body against it. James stared.

For a moment, his father was still. His face softened. James saw the man that he had loved when he was a boy. James saw the father he had been prior to his mother dying. He hadn't been perfect then, either, but compared to the last years, he was father of the year material. He had been loving. He had been someone to follow. However, once James' mother had died, his father became someone to run from.

James' face went slack and then crashed in upon itself. He made choking sounds, but no tears fell. His breath was escaping him like it was on fire. James looked at him longingly and with great sorrow.

James' father's face returned to the man he had become; the one James was all too familiar with. James' body rocked with explosion after explosion. He screamed at the cannibal animal his father now was, being held back by a cheap, thin wooden kitchen door. James stepped to the door and put his face up to the glass. He yelled. He screamed. He banged on the sides of the house with his fists and kicked the door with his feet. His words were largely indecipherable given the rage that they jetted out of his body on. The sounds of the yelling and banging only caused his father to become more frenzied and desperate to get to James in a way that he'd not done in life. He wanted James now like he'd never wanted him.

James's father's hand busted through the window and grabbed the front of James' face. He pulled James toward the window through the glass that wasn't already shattered. That glass broke around and shattered onto James's face cutting into his skin, forcing blood from beneath its surface. James shifted into panic mode and began screaming frantically and pushed himself away from the door, his father's grip and the house as much as he could to avoid the teeth of the snarling monster.

The others sprang into action, racing up the three steps to the small porch to pull James free. With their collective strength, it was done quickly with the end result of John, Lucas and Bob heaped on the broken pavement of the walkway that led from the driveway. Sandrine rushed to them, untying them from each other.

Lucas and John scrambled to look at James and assess the damage. Lucas pulled a piece of glass from the side of his nose. Blood covered James' face. They couldn't tell how badly he was hurt.

As Bob got to his feet, he looked at James' father's arm reaching out through the broken glass of the kitchen door. A long slab of fleshy muscle hung and swung as the arm waved around looking for James. He pushed against a door that had started to break free from the frame. "Guys, we gotta get out of here before he gets out!" Bob said through a gurgle that quickly became vomit decorating the sidewalk.

"He's right. James can you walk?" John asked as he and Lucas got James to his feet.

"We need to get away from here and out of his sight so that we can take a look at your face. Do you think he got you at all?" Lucas asked.

James looked back at the house through the blood that obscured his sight. He wiped his eyes and that brought great pain. He cried out. Blood cascaded down his face.

"Do you?" Lucas asked again turning James to face him.

"I don't know," James uttered almost inaudibly.

Sandrine took one of James' hands in her own and led him to the truck. Bob brought down the lift gate and got up on the bed to help James up. Sandrine scrambled up after him. She started arranging for a place for James to rest comfortably.

"Bob, you wanna drive a bit and get us away from here?" Lucas asked.

"Sure," Bob answered and hopped down.

"Sandrine go with Bob. Ride in the cab, will ya?" Lucas asked.

"I want to help James. He's my Side Hooligan."

"I know you do, but as your first Side Hooligan, I want you to be safe. Please go."

Reluctantly, she hopped down off the bed and climbed into the cab of the pickup. She scooted to the center of the bench seat and slid open the back window.

"Sandrine, can you see if there are any bandages in the glove compartment?" Lucas asked her while he continued to examine James's injuries while John looked on. "John, see what you can find back here. I know we brought some stuff. I need something to wipe his face off."

James lay back against his backpack in a front corner of the bed with his eyes closed. He cried silently with his tears joining the river of blood that had started to coagulate on his face. No one would have judged him for crying, not after this.

Bob had slowed the speed of the truck once he felt that they were away from danger. He now drove slowly down the partially dirt, partially paved lane that James' family home occupied, carefully avoiding bumps and holes. He was uncertain about where to drive to, only certain that he needed to drive away from here. So far, none of this going home stuff was working out. He didn't expect to find everything normal at his house, but disappointment at this level never occurred to him. He thought it should have.

Lucas poured water lightly over James's face. James winced. He dabbed carefully, wiping away the blood, looking for glass and anything that resembled a bite. James winced some more. He concurrently gently squeezed and opened the cuts looking for any foreign objects much like he'd seen a school nurse do after a shop accident once.

He handed back the t-shirt that John had given him and asked for another. John quickly looked through another backpack and obliged. John tried to rinse the blood off the shirt that Lucas handed him. He wrung out the bloody liquid over the side of the truck, trying to get it back to a state of absorbency for re-use. The red-tinged water flew off behind the truck, caught on the wind.

Lucas plucked another small piece of glass out of James' face gently with the tips of his fingers. It only left a small pin prick of a cut. The canvas of James' skin was marred with jagged lines all about his nose and cheeks. The lacerations in his skin were rimmed with the angry redness of having been ripped apart.

"Sandrine, any band aids up there?" Lucas asked.

Sandrine shoved a handful of fast food napkins through the split window. "This is all I could find," she said loudly.

"Good job Side Hooligan," Lucas said grabbing them. He started laying them across the cuts on James' face. The blood quickly saturated the paper, each molecule racing to the edge of the napkin where it gathered like it was a weekend party at the shore. As it did so, it adhered it to the skin on James' face.

The damage wasn't as bad as it could have been, but it still wasn't very pretty and never would be. There was a two inch or so gash running diagonally from his left eye stopping just shy of the mount of his nose. Lucas took the blood-damped shirt that John had just wrung out and wiped at the coagulated blood on James' neck, face and bare arms.

"I think you're going to be okay," Lucas told James. "I think you might even be good looking now."

James started to smile and then stopped. "That was sort of funny, but my face hurts too much to smile right now."

"Good enough," Lucas replied and pulled together the few band aids that he did have. The little packages fluttered in the breeze within his grasp as the truck moved along. Lucas scooted on his knees to the back of the cab and hit the side a couple of times and asked Bob to stop for a second so that he could put the band aids on.

Bob pulled the truck to the side of the road next to a mailbox that someone had tried to knock off the post. Instead, it held on to the dried-out wood by one steely nail. The back of the mailbox jutted out perpendicular to the short beam to which it had previously been tightly secured.

Sandrine popped her head through the window to watch what Lucas was doing and see how James was making out. Bob sat behind the wheel and scanned the area for anything that needed their attention. At the moment, it was just them on the road. The few houses around them stood still and silent. If there was another living human being anywhere near them, they were in hiding.

Bob reclined a bit and rested his wrist on the steering wheel. He flicked his fingers and stared out at the road in front of him. He wondered what he would find when they finally got to his house.

When he had left for school that last morning, his father had already left for work. His mother, older brother Jose and younger brother Diego were still in bed sleeping. Jose would be up soon to go to school. He was a freshman in college. Then his mother would wake Diego and get him off to grammar school and she would go to work. Bob was second out of the house most days. His day started early so that he could get to his high school that was twenty miles away.

That last morning, Diego was curled in a ball up by the headboard of his bed, facing the wall. He never moved when Bob was getting ready for school in the morning. Bob could sing, talk on the phone, play music, it didn't matter. He wouldn't move. The kid was a heavy sleeper. The house could fall down around him and he wouldn't wake up until he was ready to wake up.

His hair was damp from being just washed, and his skin fragranced from soap in a hot shower. His clothes were clean and smelled of fabric softener. Bob left the house without saying good-bye to anyone. He didn't want to wake anyone. He'd see them all the night before at dinner, like he always did. This morning was no different than any other morning.

Bob sat behind the wheel and stared out at the road. If anything had happened in the last few minutes, he wouldn't have known. His mind had just drifted, and he'd been far off in thought. He didn't know if he was someone that could have the audacity to hope that his family was okay. Danny did. James might have. But him? He just didn't know if he dared.

He turned and looked out at the others in the bed of the truck. Sandrine had gotten out of the cab and was back there on the bed. Bob reproached himself for essentially falling asleep on watch. He was the eyes in the front.

"Welcome back, Bob," John said softly and winked. "It's okay. I was watching."

"We got any aspirin or anything?" James asked. "My face is killing me."

"It's killing me, too," John said and playfully hit James' shoulder.

"Always the wit. Glad to see all this hasn't changed you," James shot back. "Seriously, do we have anything?"

"I don't have anything. Maybe when we get to John or Bob's house, we can get some. Can you stand it until then?" Lucas asked.

"Don't have much of a choice. I'll man up for now," James answered. "Just don't make me smile."

"So where are we going next?" Sandrine asked.

"John, why don't we head to your house first? Your mom is there with just your younger brothers," Bob offered. His suggestion was as much selfless as it was selfish. He wasn't ready to face what waited for him at his family's house. After seeing James' father, the thought was terrifying him. He didn't want to see his family that way.

"Are you sure? We could go either way at this point," John said. He thought for a moment. "I'm worried about my mom and brothers."

"Yeah, man. Let's go."

"Looks like it's decided. How far from there do you think we are?" Lucas asked.

"A month or so ago, maybe a half hour. Today? Who the fuck knows?" James said sarcastically.

"Sandrine," Lucas said with a raised eyebrow, a nod toward his charge.

"Sorry for my potty mouth, darlin'. Who knows how long it will take us now?" James corrected himself.

"I'm thinking that maybe we could pop into one of those houses and find some aspirin for your pain, James," Lucas said.

"No. Let's get going while it's still early. I can wait until we get to John's house."

"My mom will have some," John assured him.

"I'm just gonna take a quick look in one house," Lucas said.

"No, don't. You know what it's like. It's always more than what we think. Let's just get to John's house. I can wait 'til then," James implored.

"You're right. Let's go guys!" Lucas said loudly.
Bob started the truck. "John, wanna come up here and direct me?"

"Yay! That means I can stay back here with you guys," Sandrine said happily.

Lucas asked Sandrine to sit up in the corner of the bed by the truck's cab. John was in the cab with Bob and started giving directions. Although the boys saw each other frequently, it was mostly on the bus or at school. James would hang out with either Danny or John occasionally, but not that often. Other than that, they didn't know each other very well before that last day on the bus.

The drive to John's house was fairly quick. It didn't take much longer than it would have on a day before the world fell apart. The road was impassable at one point with many vehicles leading up to a bottle neck. They backed up, took a side road and then cut through a field to get back on track.

As they approached John's neighborhood, remnants of the fire that Danny's father told them about was everywhere. Everything was black and charred. Buildings were either completely or partially collapsed. Charred wood littered the road. Lucas and John got out of the truck to clear the way, moving beams, parts of walls and furniture that had fallen into the street. There were no burnt bodies, oddly enough.

John lived in the poorer part of town. It was a small neighborhood of very modest homes that had been built in the late forties, after World War II. The houses popped up to house the workers and their families for a public works project that was no longer evident and, over time, had been forgotten. Once, they were nice rows of little houses, with electricity and indoor plumbing. As the years passed, these houses had become just bare minimum affordable housing.

The neighborhood had always been kept up by the state. Lawns were mowed, streets were cleaned, dead trees were cut down. Despite such care, the neighborhood was still labeled as being for those less fortunate like the elderly, single parents and those that worked infrequently for one reason or another.

The street was quiet, eerily so. Nothing moved. Unlike other areas they'd driven through, there wasn't a lot of junk thrown all over the place. A couple of travel bags were here and there. A pillow with a large stain of blood was the most shocking thing in view. There were dark skid marks starting just after John's house and were about ten feet in length. They appeared to have been made by something with wide tires.

John's house was the third one down from the top of the street, on the left. It was a square, two-bedroom, one bath, one level, brick house with a tan door just like all the other houses. The blinds in each window were closed tightly. The door was closed.

Bob backed the truck into the short driveway, ready for a quick getaway. The driveway was just long and wide enough to accommodate one car. John tried the side door and it was locked. He went back to the truck bed and grabbed his backpack and rummaged around for his keys. Finding them at the bottom and tangled with his earphones, he pulled out the messy ball of wire and metal. He separated out the house key while leaving the remaining jumble as it was.

The key slid easily into the lock on the doorknob. Disengaging the deadbolt from the jamb higher up on the door took some jiggling and pushing in just the right place.

He slowly opened the door to a silent home. One sliver of light that snuck in along the crack of a blind had dust dancing on its ray. John entered into the kitchen stirring up a dusty waltz which resulted in a swirl of activity that followed in his wake. He walked quickly through the living room, eyes taking in clues from the state of the house. He called out for his mother and brothers but was met by silence. The others had come into the kitchen and stood awkwardly the by door.

The living room coffee table had become a makeshift dinner table, meals had been left half eaten. He walked in the small hall that led to the two small bedrooms and then would land him back in the kitchen.

The first bedroom, the smaller of the two, was his mother's. Sleeping bags and blankets were piled in a heap on the floor. It looked like some or all of his three brothers had been sleeping in there with her.

John looked into the second bedroom; the one he shared with his three younger brothers. There, two sets of bunkbeds were pushed up against opposite walls. There was a large closet in this room which was considerable for such a small house. Assorted toys were scattered across the floor with clothes mixed in the mess. Three of the four bunks had been stripped of their blankets. His 'House Proud' mother would never have allowed this to stand and risk being seen by anyone except their family.

John turned the quick corner back into the kitchen. Bob stood over the table holding a piece of paper in his hand. "It's from your mother," he said holding it out to John.

John hungrily grabbed the note and read it. "It says that the army came by and did a mandatory evacuation to a school over in Sumerduck."

"Why not someplace closer?" Bob wondered.

"How far is it?" Lucas asked.

"I don't know," John answered looking at the note. "It's dated two days after we got off the bus. I'm not sure how far it is. Maybe ten, maybe fifteen miles from here? I don't know."

They stood silently in the kitchen. No one knew what to say or suggest.

"I'm gonna grab some clean clothes and then let's head to Bob's. No need in hanging around here," John said. "James, check the medicine cabinet in the bathroom for some aspirin. I don't know what to do but it's only fair that we check out Bob's house before we do anything else."

"We don't have to. My whole family is there. They have each other," Bob responded.

"You don't want to see them? See if they're okay?" John asked.

Bob looked down at the floor.

"You okay, Bob?" Lucas asked reaching out to touch Bob's arm.

"I do want to see them," Bob croaked not looking up. "I'm scared. I don't know what I'll find when I get there." A tear that seemed to grow in mass as it slipped down over his chin splattered on the kitchen floor.

"Bob," John said but said nothing else. John clapped him on the shoulder and went back to his closet bedroom. "There might be some stuff that'll fit Sandrine if you want to look."

"That's boy's stuff. I'm not a boy," Sandrine retorted sulkily.

"You don't have much of a choice right now. You could use some extra clothes," Lucas reasoned.

"Are you going to grab some of John's mother's clothes then if she's your size?" Sandrine countered.

"No, he's not!" John yelled from the other room.

"I guess not, then," Lucas said. "I would if I needed to, though."

"I don't care. I'm not gonna!" Sandrine responded crossing her arms across her chest smugly smiling having won the battle.

Back in the truck, they headed to Bob's house. Bob was driving and taking his time doing so, at that. John sat in the cab with him. Lucas looked at Bob through the split window. He could hear John talking to him. Bob would nod, say a word or two, but otherwise stared straight at the road.

In the truck bed, James reclined with his backpack beneath his head. He was feeling better after downing some aspirin. The nerve endings in his face were sleeping.

It was late afternoon by this point in the day. It would have been dinner time before the clocks stopped ticking. The sun was creeping slowly down toward the trees like it was trying to back out of a room without anyone noticing. A military Humvee sped by them. When Bob noticed the Humvee coming, he stopped the truck hoping for any bit of information from someone in charge. Bob studied his side view mirror. The Humvee never hit the brakes.

They continued on and a little further down the road, there was a group of about ten people walking on the side of the road. Mostly women and children dragging rolling luggage behind them. That much noise wouldn't keep them safe for long.

One man walked to the side of group, toward the middle of the street. He wore a backpack and carried a rifle. He had a gun holstered on his hip. As the truck slowed on approach, the man motioned with the rifle for them to keep going. Bob and he locked eyes as they passed one another. The man's face had been freshly beaten. Blood had run from his nose and crusted on his skin. His left cheek was a plum color. Bob wondered if these people had anything to do with the military truck that sped by them. If so, maybe they were lucky that the Humvee kept going.

Sandrine looked at the people shrinking from view as the truck got further away from them. As they encountered a curve in the road, Lucas saw a zombie come out from a copse of trees headed for the travelers. The truck followed the curve and the people were history.

Bob stopped at the top of his street. The entrance to his neighborhood was impassable with a vehicle. The neighborhood had blockaded itself. There were two large trucks pulled across the opening of the street along with some sawhorses to keep anyone from entering.

Bob and his family lived in a newer housing development. It had a decorative stone wall on either side of the road that preceded the entrance to his neighborhood. The name of the development, "Pine Meadows," was engraved in bronze plaques on each side of the street.

Beyond the stone fencing lay a maze of streets that cut across one another eventually leading back out through the same opening. Upscale, mostly two-story homes were built using the same five architectural plans. Each house was colored from a limited selection of the same muted color palette that the homeowners association enforced. There would be no white houses here, just subtle earth tones. The differences between the houses came from those that lived within. Otherwise, one house was very much like the one on either side and across from it.

Bob parked the truck, got out and walked to the blockade. Leaning on the hood of one of the trucks, he looked down the street. It was devoid of anything human. There were a few cannibal animals meandering about. One in particular, headed toward the blockade looked a lot like old Mr. Thompson. It was difficult to be sure at this distance, but the yellow sweater was a signature item for the man. "Who else would wear that?" Bob thought.

Bob walked down the length of one of the trucks to climb over the tailgate to get to the other side. A wretched hand reached up from the bed of the truck and grabbed onto Bob's arm. As Bob jerked back from the surprise, he screamed, and his movement pulled the body of the cannibal animal upright. Bob's sudden movement caused his pants to fall to his ankles and they tripped him. Bob had lost weight, they all had. Bob hadn't been paying attention to his pants getting looser.

Lucas, James, Sandrine and John had already gotten out of the truck and were just feet from Bob when the attack occurred. James scooped Bob up while Lucas and John went after the monster in the truck bed. Lucas screamed for Sandrine to get back in the truck. She was locked in the cab before his last word hit her ears.

Bob stumbled getting back up, trying to pull up his jeans while James pulled him up from the ground. Lucas and John rushed to the truck bed, both with knives in hand, and began stabbing at the morbid beast. It continued to fight despite the bloody blows.

Bob watched Lucas and John struggling with the meat sack in the bed of truck. There were two young men giving it everything they had and yet, the ghoul fought. Something hit him. That ghoul, that monster was familiar to him. There was something in its appearance that Bob knew. He ran at the truck screaming for Lucas and John to stop. "That's my dad! Stop!" Bob screamed over and over again. "Oh God! Stop!

John landed the fatal blow when what Bob was screaming finally made sense to him. He dropped the bloody knife to the ground. John looked down at the knife aghast at what Bob had screamed and connected it to what he'd just done. Blood dripped from his hand, dotting the tar below. He found his voice and said, "What are you talking about? How can that," John abruptly stopped. It hit him. He had forgotten that these monsters had once been human beings, people that someone knew. These were all people that someone had known.

Seeing the knife on the ground, Bob crumpled crying and repeating over and over, "That can't be him. That can't be him. I know it isn't." It was and he knew it was. His mind suddenly raced to wondering about the rest of his family. He stood up quickly and got his pants up around his waist. We gotta go to my house. He walked around the back of the truck, climbing up on the bumper, holding onto the liftgate to slide past the point where the truck and stonewall met.

"Wait! Don't! You need a knife or gun or something," James yelled after him. "Wait for us!"

Bob looked back but kept going.

Mr. Thompson had now made it to within six feet of the pickup truck blockade and had his eyes fixed on Bob.

John and Lucas scrambled over the truck's bumper to catch up with Bob, Sandrine in tow. James climbed into the bed of truck that Bob's father lay in and brought his rifle to his shoulder. His face hurt when he squinted to take aim. One shot and Mr. Thompson's head exploded like an over-filled water balloon.

Bob didn't even flinch when a piece of skull and brain tissue hit his back. Instead, he pulled his belt tighter around his waist and trotted down the street. The other kids ran after him weaving, stabbing and knocking down the bloated cannibal animals that had come out for mealtime and excitement. There weren't very many at first, but the further they got into the neighborhood the more that surfaced.

"How much further Bob?" James yelled from behind Bob.

"That next street on the right and three houses down on the left."

Sandrine stayed close to Lucas. He wouldn't have it any other way. Since he'd found her, he had become her protector, her surrogate brother, mother and father. They made their way chasing after Bob doing their one-two routine. One, she would knock them down if she could and then two, he would put a knife in the eye socket or temple. It worked perfectly when there weren't too many. They had been lucky. They had never encountered too many at a time.

Sandrine had just finished knocking down a woman by kicking her in the back of the knees when a little girl ghoul with shoulder length brown hair appeared in the wake of the woman's fall. Their eyes locked. Lucas screamed for her to get out of the way. Sandrine stood transfixed on this little monster that not too long ago had been playing with her friends. Sandrine wondered if this former pre-tween had loved Elmo as much as she did. Sandrine wondered if she had just knocked down the girl's mother. Sandrine wondered at how the girl ended up like this with half her arm missing and covered in blood. Sandrine was suddenly yanked sharply snapping her out of her trance by Lucas. "Stick with me!" He yelled at her.

Up ahead Lucas saw a clear street and the other three boys rounding a corner. "Hurry!" Lucas yelled at Sandrine, holding her little hand in his as she struggled to match the strides that his five-foot ten-inch frame made.

As Lucas and Sandrine turned the corner onto Bob's street, they saw John scrapping with one of the things. Arms swinging, heads bobbing while John tried to land his knife. James came up behind the cannibal animal, pulled its head back, cradled it in the crook of his arm while he drove his seven-inch Bowie knife into its temple. He dropped someone's grandpa to the ground and asked John if he was okay.

Bob was at the front door of the house. He tried the knob and it was locked. He bent and lifted the door mat and found the housekey. He slid the key into the two locks on the door and pushed it open and yelled for his family. There was no caution in him, just urgency. Silence greeting him. "Mom?" He yelled even louder. Again, silence.

"They can hear you all the way back to the truck!" James said quietly behind him. "Hurry up and get in here before they find us!" He said turning to address the others.

They all stood in the foyer of Bob's family home. The staircase landed right in front of them. The living room to the left was in perfect order. The dining room to the right had stockpiles of supplies lined along the walls. Water, loose and boxed canned food, jugs, blankets and two boxes with pictures of tents on the outside of them was just a taste of what had been collected. On the table lay a shotgun with ten boxes of shells sitting next to it.

"Hello?" Bob said as he walked by the staircase using the hall that led to the kitchen. The others followed. There was no answer. The kitchen counters were covered with opened and empty cans. Ants and assorted other bugs were having a full-on festival celebrating the abundance of abandoned food left out to delight their appetites.

Lucas walked to the counter and looked into some of the cans. "I don't think these have been sitting here for very long. Maybe they're not far."

"I know where my dad is. The rest of my family could be out there, too," Bob answered.

"We don't know that. It looks like someone was eating here not too long ago. The tuna left in this can isn't dried out yet," James said.

At hearing that, Bob ran to the basement door and down the stairs screaming, "Hello? Is anyone here?" with John chasing after him. Their feet hit each step sounding like boulders bouncing down the side of a mountain.

Lucas and James started moving through the first floor of the house searching the rooms and opening closet doors. The house definitely had signs of recent occupancy, but the question really was how recent and what had become of the occupants?

Bob and John were conducting the same sort of search except Bob was gathering things and shoving them into John's hands, as well. When John's burden became too great, he walked it over to the bottom of the basement stairs.

Sandrine waited in the kitchen while the others searched the house. She started cleaning up by grabbing an empty box and throwing the empty cans and wrappers into it. She dragged a kitchen island bar stool over to the counter and climbed up on it. She knelt on the seat and opened the cabinet doors in front of her, leaning back a bit to do it, looking for food. She heard the clang of pans shifting in a cabinet below. She froze and listened. Silence. She resumed her search, pulling cans of food out of the cabinet. She heard it again and froze.

Slowly and as quietly as she could, Sandrine got down from the counter. She tip-toed over to the large cabinet under the kitchen island and stood in front of it. She slowly opened the cabinet door to see a dark head of curly hair helmeted around the biggest blue eyes that she'd ever seen.

"Hi," the little boy said softly, his mouth barely moved.

"Hi," Sandrine said back. "My name is Sandrine. Do you live here?"

"Yes."

"Bob!" Sandrine yelled and all the boys came running.

Bob hit the top of the steps to see his little brother emerging from the cabinet. He slid on his knees across the wood floor to embrace him. Tears fell from Bob's eyes and soaked the shoulder of his brother's t-shirt.

"Bob?" the little boy started, "you don't smell very good."

"That makes two of us. You smell like crap, Diego," he responded and chuckled through his tears. "What have you been doing?"

The boy broke into a wide gaping smile revealing that his two front teeth were missing and said, "Not taking baths!"

"Obviously," Bob said amid the laughter of the group. Bob sat on the kitchen floor looking at his little brother, relieved to find someone in the house after seeing what had become of his father. He knew he must ask where the rest of their family was.

This question was being answered over and over on this trip. Danny's family was all still alive or at least they were when they left him. His father had been bitten. He was likely gone now. James' father had joined the cannibal animal parade. John's mother and brothers were at a refugee camp, if they even made it. Now, it was Bob's turn.

"Where is mom and Jose, Diego? Are they around?"

"People came here. They wanted to come in. Mom and Jose went outside with dad a while ago. They didn't come back."

"Okay. They still must be out there," Bob said just above a whisper.

James put his hand on Bob's shoulder to comfort him. They all suspected what happened, but still weren't sure. How could they give any comfort for this? Bob's father had turned, and it was possible that his mother and brother had experienced the same fate, as well. Otherwise, they would be here with Diego right now.

"Why were you hiding in the cabinet?" Lucas asked. "Mom told me to hide and not come out until they came back. So, I did."

"What happened?" Bob asked.

"I don't know," Diego said as he started to cry.

"Hey, hey, hey big guy," Bob said as he pulled Diego into his arms and held him tightly as he rocked him a bit. "I'm here. I'm here. I got you. Please don't cry."

Sandrine made a raspberry noise and broke out in sobs. Within seconds, they were all crying in a huddled mess on the floor loosely intertwined with one another.

James lay back on the floor and gingerly wiped at his eyes. "My tears are stinging my cuts."

Lucas looked at him, "We should see what they have here. Bob? Aspirin in medicine cabinets?"

"Probably that and more," Bob croaked. "Guys, I can't leave here."

"I don't wanna go!" Diego protested

"You can't stay here," James and John said in unison.

"Not with so many of them outside," James said.

"Maybe not, but I can't leave here until I know about my mom and older brother."

Lucas stood up, wiping his face of tears with his dirty, blood-stained t-shirt, "We don't have to leave right away, but the guys are right. There's too many of them wandering around out there."

"I'll think about it," Bob answered.

He was inside the house. He didn't know quite what to make of it. They were all gone, and they took the little girl, Sandrine with them. The house was neat. It didn't appear that they'd left in a hurry. Maybe they would be coming back.

He carved his name inside one of the cabinet doors. He brushed the wood fragments into his hand and then dumped them just outside the door into the overgrown flowerbed.

He found the room and the bed that he thought that she slept in. The one with the doll must be hers. He pulled back the blankets and crawled beneath them, pulling them all the way to his chin. He turned his head and forced his nose down into the pillow and inhaled deeply. He could smell her. The pillowcase smelled slightly of sweat and of shampoo and little girl, he thought. The scents were faint. He touched himself through his pants until he grew hard, solid. He rubbed and he stroked until his crotch was wet and then he lay there.

It was time to get back home. He needed to get her a squirrel, a dog, a woman or something. He had to bring her something. He had found her a fancy leather collar during his foraging. He couldn't wait to put it on her. She was going to love it! She was the dog he never had, but always wanted.

Lizzie stood at the kitchen sink looking out of the window at the back yard and the shed where her parents lay wrapped in blankets and covered with tarp. No one buys a shed thinking it will be a tomb for their eternal rest. Tree branches heavy with leaves swayed over it like they were swishing away the smell of decay.

It had been three days since they'd met Chuck and his family. It was Chuck's family that haunted Lizzie. He had lost his entire family. All of it. All gone! All monsters! She feared that each expired day brought her closer to the same fate. Mike was already gone, turned and then, ended. Lizzie had been looking for nearly a week for the girls and had seen nothing, not a trace. What if her girls were already gone? All gone? All monsters?

"Okay, I'm ready." Kenya said entering the kitchen knocking Lizzie out of the barrage of her worrisome thoughts.

Lizzie went to Kenya and hugged her. Kenya needed it and Lizzie needed some affection, too. This was lonely, scary business these days. She had heard Kenya crying this morning. She hated that Kenya would carry the memory of the rape the rest of her life. It wasn't something you forgot no matter how much you wish that you would. Lizzie blamed herself for not knowing what lay within the breast of Mr. Harvey all those years. Lizzie blamed herself for not stopping it sooner. Lizzie blamed herself for not being able to take the pain from Kenya. "Where's your jacket sweetie?"

"Lizzie, have you felt the air? It's like seventy something today already. You won't need that warehouse coat of yours. You ready? Let's go," Kenya said heading out of the back door to a Honda parked behind the house. Lizzie grabbed her big coat anyway. She didn't like to be cold and after all, it had those great pockets where she could put all her secrets.

"How much gas in the car?" Lizzie called after the girl. They'd found the Honda on the way back after meeting Chuck. Keys in the ignition and gas in the tank, an easy score, it gave them a ride home.

"I think just under a half. Enough to look around a bit if we don't go too far. Can I drive?" Kenya asked with a hopeful smile.

Lizzie nodded her assent, smiling to herself as she followed Kenya.

They were somewhere between where they'd found the abandoned Buckner family SUV and Lizzie's parent's house. They'd been driving down route 17 back toward home when they'd taken a side street looking for the girls, primarily, along with scavenging gas and various other sundries, secondarily. From the look of the map this road would sweep back around to route 17 after a mile or so.

Fields and houses set far apart made up the landscape of both sides of the road that the Honda traveled. It was a real country setting. There weren't many houses. Some homesteads had barns and large garages. There were a couple of large gardens that had been started not too long ago. That was something to keep note of for food when it was ready.

The area was quiet and eerily clear of cannibal animals. They remarked to one another about this and wondered if the people had been evacuated. They stopped at one house set back from the road because there was a tractor in the side yard next to a plowed field. There were also a few outbuildings. "Lots of possibilities for scavenging here," Lizzie thought to herself.

Lizzie had managed to siphon out almost ten gallons of gas from the four vehicles on the property including the tractor which had been almost empty but still yielded well over two gallons. She put the plastic jugs in the trunk of the Honda and headed to the barn to find Kenya.

Kenya was standing at a workbench. She had an array of gardening implements set out. She picked one up, swung it around and pantomimed trying to take down a dead head and then moved on to another one and did the same. When Lizzie walked in, Kenya narrowly missed jabbing Lizzie through the jaw with a pitchfork.

"Find anything good?" Lizzie asked as she approached, bobbing backward quickly to avoid being impaled.

"Well, I'm trying to decide if one of these things would be better than a knife. I want some distance," she responded as she turned and leaned the pitchfork against the bench and picked up a garden trawl. She swiped it through the air like it was a bear's claw. "What do you think of this?" She asked. "Do you think this would be getting too close? I think it's still too close."

"I think it might depend on skill, confidence and luck. It might not be too easy to pull something like that out quickly if there's more than one of them," Lizzie surmised as she looked it over and thought for a second. "But, ya know, it's probably a lot easier to carry around than a pitchfork." She paused again and then continued, "A pitchfork would be perfect for someone that was short and couldn't really reach up that far. Now, that could be a marvelous thing."

"Marvelous? Did you just say marvelous?" Kenya asked laughing. "Why didn't you just say, 'Darling, you would look absolutely marvelous skewering a dead head with a pitchfork. It's all the rage in Milan this year!" Kenya said affecting a hoity toity-type accent and swinging the pitchfork. By this point, Lizzie was laughing at her, nearly in tears and grabbing her belly.

"Well, I like both of these things. I'm gonna take them," Lizzie said and grabbed a scythe with a short handle and a pitchfork. "I want to check out the house across the street real quick and pick some lilacs. There are a ton of bushes over there and those are my favorite flowers. Everything stinks to high heaven. I hope those flowers still smell like lilacs. Plus, who knows if I'll ever see them again?"

Kenya grabbed the other pitchfork from the barn, propped it against the Honda next to the one that Lizzie had placed there. She followed Lizzie across the street.

This house had an expanse of land just like the one they had just come from. They poked about inside the house a bit and put together a large canvas tote bag of miscellaneous goods and left it outside the front door. Lizzie handed Kenya a sweater commenting on the air having gotten cooler and that she was glad that she had her jacket and joked that age often equals wisdom and wrinkles.

They walked to the side yard where there was a small shed and behind that a wall of tall lilac bushes in a mixed pattern of light purple and white flowers. They could smell the scent of the blooms long before they reached the bushes. Yes, the perfume delightfully offset the stench of the dead.

Lizzie walked right up to the bushes and buried her nose in the petals breathing in their essence as deeply as she could. For a few brief moments, everything was normal and beautiful. There were no dead walking the Earth. There weren't rapists. She wasn't a murderer. Mike, Kevin, and Hershey were still alive. Her girls weren't lost. She was just someone caught in the reverie of pulling the lilac scent into the depths of her lungs on a sunny day.

She reached out and started breaking off branches here and there putting together a bouquet. Kenya was further ahead of her walking along the line of bushes. She disappeared and then popped out again.

"Lizzie, come look at this!" She said in a raised voice just below yelling.

Lizzie walked up to meet Kenya and saw that there was a keyhole doorway formed by the bushes that created an entry way to the other side. Beyond the doorway there was another field filled with high grass and a small house off in the distance. They both went through and started walking along the wall of lilacs. Lizzie continued to pick blooms of both colors. She had assembled quite a large bouquet by this point.

"Look what I found," Kenya said coming up behind her holding a teddy bear and brushing off dirt, twigs and ground debris.

Lizzie turned toward her, saw what was in Kenya's hand, dropped the flowers and ripped the bear out of Kenya's hands. It was worn in all the places she remembered, the one button eye she had sewn on, the clump of black thread that was the original eye and both ears frayed around the edges. The tan belly still had its mismatched patch low on the abdomen and the leg that had been sewn back on when Hershey had chewed it off. This bear, Kiko, had begun life with Margaret but somehow ownership had peacefully transferred to Olivia and Olivia was never without this bear. Lizzie ran her hand over Kiko's belly as if to check if it was real.

"It's Kiko. Where did you find this?" Lizzie asked anxiously.

"About twenty feet down that way by the bushes," Kenya responded as she turned and pointed.

"This is Olivia's," Lizzie said excitedly as she looked up at Kenya and started to scan the fields. All she could see were overgrown grasses, the tops of the shafts swaying in response to the light breeze blowing across them. Then she saw it, a head of red hair pop out of an opened door. From this distance, that red hair looked like it was bobbing just above the grass. A second head of dirty blonde hair popped out behind the first one. "My girls!" Lizzie shouted. "Kenya, look!"

Their attention was immediately drawn to the sound of a vehicle approaching them. A beat-up work pickup truck with "Fuller and Son Roofing" printed on the side pulled into the driveway of the house they had just scavenged. It parked near the bag of their newly found goods. Dust swirled around the truck as the doors opened and out came four men and woman from the cab and two more men jumping over the sides of the bed. Lizzie and Kenya dropped down and watched them through the lilac bushes.

All were armed with rifles, handguns and some knives, save the woman. All she carried were the clothes on her back, and her bruised and cut face. Where the men talked and bickered amongst themselves, the woman was silent and dour.

It was evident that this group was living the rough nomadic life. They were dirty and disheveled, the woman especially. She wore a hooded sweatshirt that was ripped as if it had been torn from her and when she walked, she gripped it about herself.

She walked slowly and with a slight limp over to the canvas bag of goodies. She bent over sifting through the contents and from time to time, stood up as straight as she could to examine one of the finds. It was one of those times that one of the men walked over to her and stood with the butt of his rifle resting on his hip. He pulled a flask from his back pocket, took a swig and returned it. He then slapped the can she was holding out of her hands and then slapped the back of her head. She instinctively brought her hands and arms up to shield her head as she crouched down.

"Knock it off Billy!" One of the men yelled. "She's almost worn out as it is. I was hoping this one would last a little bit longer. We'll be lucky to get another go at this rate."

"Yeah, Billy! It's been a little slow without your mother around," A second one yelled.

Billy turned and shot a bullet near the feet of the second man and they all laughed.

"Sssh!" Kenya said putting her fingers up to her lips. "Come look!" She whispered.

"Shit," Lizzie said staring at the grizzly group. "My girls," she said as she continued to survey the situation. "I can't risk my girls."

"Maybe if we just wait here, they'll move on."

"I can't risk my girls," Lizzie turned to Kenya, "Listen to me. Go get my girls. Hide them. When it's safe, take them back to the house. I'll meet you there when I can."

"We can't separate. We need to stick together."

"I don't think we can. If you go to my girls and hide them, then I can distract these guys if I have to and you can get away. If I don't have to, I'll meet you back at the house," Lizzie said studying the group. "I promise. I'll be there before long," Lizzie said placing her hand on Kenya's head to assure her.

"I'll just wait with you."

No. We can't risk it," Lizzie said as she turned to look at Kenya. "No! Listen to me," Lizzie said sternly, "They look like bad folks, and if they are, and if you stay, they could get us both and my girls will still be out here on their own. I don't want that. Go get my girls so you can lead them back to the house and I will meet you there. Do you understand?"

Kenya looked at her and said nothing. She knew Lizzie was right, but she didn't want to separate. She was scared.

"Look, sweetie, you can do this. Look at me," Lizzie said sternly again. "You are mine now. I love you. You can do this. I'm trusting you to do this," she paused and said pleadingly, grabbing Kenya's hands, "I need you to do this." Lizzie gave her one more beseeching look, handed her Kiko and said firmly, "Now go!"

Kenya stood in a crouch and started running through the field trying to keep her head from being too far above the top of the grass. She did her best to run as fast as she could. Lizzie watched her go with deep apprehension, sadness, hope, and relief.

When Kenya's head was far enough away so that it just bobbed above the top of the tall grass, Lizzie turned to watch the proceedings on the other side of the bushes. The men had spread out a bit and one was inside the shed near the wall of lilacs. She couldn't see him, but she could hear him throwing things around while he searched. Metal clanging and things hitting the wooden floor.

Lizzie knew she was only safe where she was as long as no one came too close to the bushes or the keyhole doorway. She crouched looking through the lilac branches watching the men. Lizzie started moving backwards in a crouching position into the grass behind her. As she shifted weight from one foot to the other, she stepped back on uneven ground and lost her balance. Her arm went out to stop her fall, but she leaned too far over and her jumble of keys fell out of her pocket in a seemingly thundering crash of tinkling metal. Instantly she dropped as low as she possibly could and prayed that the Earth would swallow her up. For an eternity she heard silence.

Silence never lasts when you want it to. There was the crunch of boots on pebbly dirt and a deep voice above her and then she was flying.

Fear, Grief and Terror

"At least I wasn't afraid to be born alone!" Olivia retorted sarcastically.

"Only because you ate your twin!" Margaret shot back. "When you were born Mom cried every day because of you!"

"Take that back!" Olivia screamed as she pounced on Margaret and pummeled her with tiny balled up fists.

Margaret had retreated into a defensive ball with her arms up in front of her.

They were hiding in a busted-up minivan on the side of the road. They had crawled in to hide from a group of about twenty cannibal animals that they'd encountered while looking for a vehicle and their grandparent's house. They had had sat on the floorboards silently waiting for them to pass.

"Stop it you guys! Stop it!" Lucy hissed as she came running over to break the two of them apart. "Do you want them to hear us?" She asked looking at the girls. "We managed to outrun a pack of them and get in here. They can't be far away."

Both girls stared back her with wide, horrified eyes. They didn't want that.

They had been wandering for the last week trying to get to their grandparent's house. They had been looking for a car to drive but couldn't find anything unlocked, with keys, and gas.

They had walked and stopped and walked and stopped down a long country lane mostly lined with trees. A house, a shack, a clearing, a dirt road would pop up on either side of them. It was at a gathering of large rocks that their lackadaisical day changed.

Margaret had been complaining of something in her sneaker hurting her foot for a while. Lola had kept her walking for as long as she could until they came to a bunch of large rocks at the end of a dirt driveway.

"Let's eat since we're stopping again," Lucy said emphasizing the word again. "Nana and Poppup's house is around here somewhere."

They huddled together on the cropping of stones. Margaret got the stone out of her shoe. Lola and Lucy sparingly doled out crackers and slices of pepperoni. Olivia complained that she wanted more. Lola told her that they all did, but until they got to Nana and Poppup's they were watching what they had.

They sat silently, each in her own thoughts. Olivia had crumbs cascading down the front of her t-shirt. She stared blankly at the street. Margaret had reclined completely on her rock. Her feet were on the ground and her body surrendered to the convex curve of the rock; blood rushed to her upside-down head.

Lucy sat hunched over, head in hands, slowly munching on her slice of pepperoni. She pulled the casing off with her teeth, rolled it around in her mouth feeling the smooth plastic-like film and sucked on it. She tasted the spice and tang of the meat on her tongue. Lucy was absolutely intent on savoring every burst of flavor. It was such a little slice and would soon be gone, possibly forever. "What if this is the last time I eat pepperoni?" She asked herself.

There was a crack of a twig, some dried up and fragile piece of woodsy carpet. Lucy jerked her head up, looking around. She inhaled deeply and smelled the death around them.

"We gotta go, I think," said Lola.

A, "Grrrrr," met Lola's words and then they appeared. Four former men lumbered out from the brush about twenty feet away.

"The funny thing about cannibal animals," Margaret thought, "was that they didn't care about briars like real people did."

Those monsters just pushed right through them like they were silky ribbons covered in velvet. The walking idiots felt none of the pricks and scrapes from the vine-hung thorns. One of them was draped in the thorny vines like Christmas garland on a tree. The vine was still entangled with the brush that it had walked through creating a clothesline scenario. It tried to pull itself forward, but it was just stuck. Margaret stared dumbly at it. A second cannibal animal appeared beside the first and tripped over one of the lower vines pulling the first one with him to the ground. Margaret giggled. They both struggled to regain their feet. The two others passed by them unimpeded.

Lola grabbed Margaret and Margaret's bag and started pulling her along, telling her to put her bag on her back.

"Come on you guys!" Lucy hissed. She had Olivia by the hand. The two had made it back to the street. "we can outrun them. Let's go!"

The four girls hustled down the street. Each looking for a place to hide. The four grotesque ogres quickly turned into ten. One was much closer than they liked; they all were. However, the one out front was particularly intent on snaring its next meal.

The Dad Bod cannibal animal's full belly was eclipsed by the overwhelming amount of blood that drenched the front of its shirt and pants. There was so much blood, it couldn't be discerned if there was a bite and if there was, where it was.

Margaret looked back and saw the cannibal animal in the lead. A low moan crawled in her throat.

"Don't worry, M. You guys'll be okay," Mike assured her. He trotted backward in front of her.

"Think you guys can push it? I think I see something up ahead," Lucy said.

"C'mon lard butt!" Mike yelled good-naturedly. He turned around and ran beside Margaret. "We gotta get it in gear."

"Ok," Margaret replied.

"Ok?" Lola asked.

"Yeah, let's pick it up. Let's go!" Margaret huffed and broke into a run. For possibly the first time ever, Margaret was pulling Lola along. Enough so, that they were keeping pace with Lucy and Olivia.

"Here!" Lucy yelled. She looked back for Lola and Margaret to find them right beside her and Olivia. Lucy could also see that there were very likely more than ten cannibal animals after them now. She couldn't exactly count them, but she did see some she hadn't seen before.

They ran down a long dirt driveway that lead to a house. Just a simple house. They tried the front door and it was locked. Lucy looked down the length of the driveway to see that Dad Bod was leading the pack and they were starting to make their way down the drive. Now was the time to hide while they still might have a slight advantage. "Follow me," she instructed her younger sisters. Lucy ran toward the wall of lilac bushes that lined one side of the house's yard. If she could get her sisters through those bushes then she could put some distance between themselves and the monsters chasing them.

They got across the lawn and ran along the bushes looking for a way through and found this interesting break that was shaped like a door. Once through, they were met with a field of high grass beyond which a white house beckoned to them from the other side. Lucy grabbed Olivia's hand and yanked her suddenly along. When that happened, little Kiko, Olivia's and once Margaret's, beloved little bear fell out of Olivia's unzipped backpack. They left him behind on the ground at the base of the beautiful lilac bushes.

They ran across the deep field and made it to the neighboring house. They ran around to the front of the large house. It had a long wraparound porch. Some white rocking chairs lay on their sides up against the front door. They stopped short at the steps to the porch.

Looking across, back at the lilac wall, Lola saw that Dad Bod and his army had made it that far and were now trapped. Some had been knocked to the ground and started crawling through beneath the bushes and between the skinny trunks. Other's had found the break in bushes and were now making their way through the tall grass.

"Maybe if we go in the house, hide and be quiet, they'll forget about us," Lola suggested. "Out of sight, out of mind."

"She's on to something and you guys could use a rest," Mike said.

"Right. She's right," Margaret said.

"What's gotten into that girl?" Lola asked looking at Lucy and marveling that there wasn't a complaint or an argument, but agreement coming from Margaret.

"No time to find out," Lucy answered while running up the front steps to try the front door. She pushed one of the rockers out of the way and tried the wooden framed screen door and it was locked. She turned, coming back down the steps, wading through her sisters that had followed her.

"Try the side or back door," Mike suggested. "There's another way in."

Margaret nodded and suggest that they do just that. The pack of four ran toward the back of the house. They spotted a side door to the house. A few wooden steps led up to a black door framing beveled glass panels. From somewhere inside, perhaps a window, light shone through the glass.

"Wait a sec. I'll try this door," Lola said as she ran up the three steps and tried the knob. It turned easily and she slowly pushed the door open. "Anyone in here?" Lola asked and her ears were met with silence.

Lucy could see heads and some shoulders making their way through the field. She turned to see Lola as she stood agog at the end of the hallway looking into a room. She ran up the steps and down the hall to join her. "What is it?" Lucy asked on approach and then saw it.

It was unlike anything they had ever seen in the brief history of their sheltered, complacent American lives. A family or what they assumed was a family lay torn apart in some type of drama on display in what was likely the 'good' room of the house that was only used for best company.

Pale dusky rose carpet, white furniture, a giant grandfather clock were all lit by a sun's rays that filtered through the giant bow window that showcase the best of the front lawn's landscaping in better days.

Lucy put out her hand to stop her two younger sisters from advancing any further. The last thing they needed to see was this diorama of horror. Blood was splashed and splattered over every conceivable surface. The rug was a deep crimson in places where pools of sticky matter gathered. The white furniture looked as if Jackson Pollack had stopped by for an afternoon of fun.

An axe handle stood sticking straight up with the blade firmly planted into a toddler's head. The toddler was missing most of a leg. A woman, presumably the mother, lay prone with arms outstretched reaching out to the child. A bullet wound having taken off a significant portion of her head. One could conclude she was no longer worried about the child.

On the opposite side of the room, sprawled over one of the easy chairs was a body whose sex could not be discerned. Its body was supine, and the head was bent so far back over the arm of the chair that the neck had to be broken. The toddler's leg was on the floor just below the arm of the body in the chair. The bloodied hand was draped over the armrest and opened, hanging over the leg as if it had dropped it.

"There's no way to close this off," Lola said while looking for doors.

"Guys don't come any closer," Lucy warned.

The girls didn't listen and crept closer until both sets of eyes peeked around the corner. Margaret quickly turned and moved hastily back down the hall and out the door with Olivia behind her. Neither girl bothered to look for an all clear. What they'd seen inside that house was worse and first in their mind over what was steadily creeping its way across the field.

Once out of the house, all four girls stood at the bottom of the steps in the dirt. Lola spotted a head above the grass and saw that Dad Bod was making good time. She looked around at all the artifacts of a family gathered around the steps. "Guys! Pick something up and throw it into the grass toward the back of the house. Quick! Maybe they will follow that," Lola ordered.

Each of the girls picked up something and threw it as far as they could into the long grass. Margaret grunted as she threw a rock that was too big for her. She threw it and it didn't go very far. Olivia threw a plastic truck that landed just into the grass line. Lucy hit the jack pot. She found a small firetruck with an on button for sound. She pushed the button, the siren sounded loudly. She walked up to the grass line and she miraculously threw the firetruck about twenty or thirty feet away from her, still deep into the field.

The firetruck had sunk into the grass and the siren continued to wail. The girls could see that this had done the trick as the mob started to veer toward the siren call and away from them.

"Quick! Let's get down the driveway and outta here!" Lola yelled, and the girls started to run to the front of the house.

"Wait," a woman said. She was wearing a bedraggled lavender knit hat and emerged from the tall grass. She had a scratch on her face that was bleeding. She held a finger over her mouth and said, "Don't scream. Your mother sent me," Kenya held out Kiko toward Oliva as she advanced. "I found this."

The girls stopped in their tracks looking at the stranger that came bearing the bear that had been recently been lost along with a claim that their mother sent her to them. They were puzzled and surprised and elated all at once.

Lola pointed to the remnants of the herd still moving toward the siren in the tall grass and whispered, "We can't stay here."

"You're right, we can't. We need to get to your grandparent's house."

"Who are you?" Margaret asked.

"I'm Kenya. We need to put some distance between us and those flesh-eating robots. Follow me."

They slept for two nights in Bob's house. They watched the neighborhood by day light looking for a large enough clearing of the dead in order to make their escape. There were still too may zombies milling about to make a run for it. There was only one way in and one way out of the cul-de-sac. The developers had nestled this little clump of homes right into a dense bed of trees not connected to any other streets.

On the third day, Lucas and James assessed the risk. They looked out of the windows on each side of the house. They counted four or five walking dead neighbors on each side.

"What do you think?" Bob asked coming up behind them in the living room.

"We were just discussing that," James replied.

"Oh, shit," Bob whispered. "That's Jose." Bob looked at his brother walked down the street in front of the family home. One sneaker was missing as was a large part of his scalp. He was a mess. His pants were ripped and bloody where someone had ripped into his thigh. Jose now walked with a very pronounced limp. "I can't take any more of this!" Bob screamed. Jose stopped and looked at the house. He slowly turned his body and began shuffling toward the house. Others slowly started to join him.

"I hate to say it, but this gives me an idea," Lucas said. "Why don't we stand in the window and scream? They'll all come over and we'll sneak out the back of the house, go through the backyards until we can get to the street."

"That could work," James responded.

"I can't leave him like that," Bob said through tears. "And I don't know what happened to my mom."

"I know, but we have an opportunity to get out of here before we are out there, like them," Lucas said pointing that the gathering group of zombies.

"I know," Bob croaked. "Let's get ready to go."

"Then we're gonna scream like hell," James said looking at Jose.

The boys got the younger kids suited up with backpacks and made sure that they weren't too heavy. Sandrine was relieved to be getting out of Bob and Diego's house. She wanted to go back to the Side Hooligan hang out house.

The boys had packed canned goods and water in their backpacks. They were definitely carrying heavy loads. They surmised that all they had to do was to get back to the truck that wasn't too far away. It was just down the street. "Hop, skip and a jump," Bob said to quell Diego's anxiety. Sandrine assured him that all would be fine, that she'd done this a million times. Lucas smirked at her confidence and loved her for it.

Sandrine and Diego were positioned at the back door, out of sight and ready to make a run for it when the conditions were just right. Lucas, James, John and Bob went to the living room windows. James and John struggled to open the two large windows next to the big picture window. Bob had to show them that these opened by sliding the tops down.

Jose had meandered back out to the street and was nowhere in sight. A few other cannibal animals milled about in front of the house. Lucas went to the door and put his hand on the doorknob. "We ready?"

"On the count of three. One. Two. Go!" Bob yelled.

Lucas whipped open the front door and the other boys started yelling as loud as they could.

"Hey! Hey, you!" John called and the neighbor stopped and looked toward the house. "I wish I could read what that t-shirt says?"

"That's Mr. Smith," Bob said, standing next to John yelling out the same window, "he would give kids candy."

"Aw sorry, man. That's kind of creepy when you think about it," John said and then yelled, "it sucks that you were all people!"

John went on a tirade about how much all this really sucks, in his opinion. He had a lifestyle that he was no longer living, after all.

"Hey, you big bag of puss! Why don't you come over here and take a big bite out of me? I'm right here," James yelled.

It was starting to work. Jose had come around the corner. Others filtered out from side yards, nooks and crannies. They weren't up at the house yet, but they were coming.

"Jackhammer jaw! Don't stand there flappin' ya gums," Bob screamed at one of the neighbors. He wondered if it was one of the neighbors or one of the people that invaded the neighborhood. He'd never know. He didn't know all the neighbors.

"What are we calling these things?" James asked.

"I've been calling them zombies. I saw something like this in a movie once," Lucas yelled out the door.

"You're an ignorant flesh bag bastard!" James yelled.

"Ya big clap-jawed flesh compactor! I'm right here and I've got the A1 steak sauce!" Lucas yelled.

"What the fuck did you just say?" Bob asked through laughter.

"I don't know. I'm just trying to say anything," Lucas responded. "I was at school, you motherless half-brained, dizzy idiot! I was going to be an architect, you asshole!"

"I wanted to graduate high school," James yelled. "How am I gonna do that? I wanted to get out of this fucking town and have a life!"

"I can't think about everything that I've lost right now. I just want to get out of here and there aren't enough of them yet. They're coming, though," John said. "You know what? You look like something the cat dragged in!" He yelled trying to bring back some levity.

"That's the best you can do?" Lucas said chuckling. "Hey, you half-witted hell shell!"

"That's a good one. I like that. Hell shell, come on over here!" Bob yelled. "There's Jose. Jose! Jose! I love you. Even like this, I love you, brother."

"Sorry, man," John said, "if nothing else, you know where he is."

"Yep, but still don't know about my mom."

"I think we've got a lot of them out there now. We just need them to get up to the windows and we can go," James observed. "You fucking drunken corpulent sock," James yelled to a particularly portly man. "Why don't you come get your next meal here?"

"Do you guys realize that we are fast food hanging out these windows?" John asked. "You know like drive-through window?"

"You just think of that?" Bob asked and then screamed from surprise. A hand slapped against the window. The cannibal animal had slipped around the side of the house and had squeezed in around the shrubbery.

"You alright?" John asked. Bob nodded yes.

"This is it guys. There's a bunch coming. Let's get them up here!" James yelled.

The boys started yelling anything they could think of. Lucas shut and locked the door. He went to the kitchen to check on

Sandrine and Diego. He told them they'd be leaving soon and to be ready. He went back to the living room and shared a window with James.

They all started screaming insults, demands and hurts at the monsters on the lawn. Slowly, the front yard was teeming with them. They limped, crawled shuffled to the front of the house so very hungry for what was inside.

Bob saw some familiar faces that had were distorted by violence or death. It made him sad. He had lived in this neighborhood since Diego had been born. Some of these people weren't very welcoming at first. Over time, things changed. There were block parties and barbeques. They got to know each other. This was home. *Was* being the operative word here. He didn't know what it was now other than it was no longer home.

"Guys, think this is enough?" James asked.

Another hand slapped the window that Bob and John occupied. The glass broke and a severed finger flew in between the two boys and landed on the carpet in front of the coffee table.

"Yeah, I think we're good. Let's go!" John yelled.

The boys ran into the kitchen and pulled on their backpacks. Bob reminded Diego and Sandrine that they were to stay in the middle of the group and to stay quiet. He did his best to pump up Diego. He was trying his best not to look scared, but it was written all over his face.

"Stick with me. I know how to handle these stiffs," Sandrine told Diego confidently.

"I think that was the one thing we didn't call them while we were yelling out those windows," James commented and gave her a high five. "Good one!"

They stepped out into the small mudroom that led to the back patio. Through the sliding glass doors, they could see that the backyard was empty. They all held some type of knife in their hand, even eight-year-old Diego. Lucas opened the door and led the way. John followed him. Sandrine and Diego were next out. James and Bob brought up the rear.

They made it out of the backyard and across three others without incident. They were hustling along with mostly the soft jingling from their gear. Sandrine didn't like the way her backpack bounced on her back. It was when they were going down the side yard of the third house that Diego tripped and cried out. Bob scooped him up and got him moving again.

As they hit the street, a lady with curlers in her hair popped out from behind a Buick parked in a driveway. She was missing most of her right hand. James looked at her as they ran by. She reached out with her left hand. In slow motion, James looked at her ring finger and the world closed in around the wedding rings. Dark, crimson blood glittered in the sunlight all around the diamond.

"I think that walking bag of flesh wants a piece of you," Bob quipped.

"Wantin' ain't gettin'," James answered and ran on.

The Side Hooligans made it to the entrance of the cul-de-sac without problem. A few of the cannibal animals had either strayed away from the house or never made it there to begin with. They trailed the group as they moved quickly along the quiet street.

"Oh, shit. Shit. Shit," Lucas said quietly as he climbed over the bumpers of the trucks. "The pickup is gone." He turned and helped Sandrine and Diego down. "They must have hot-wired it. I still have the keys in my pocket."

"We'll be okay. We'll find something else," John said.

"Yeah, but we left stuff in that truck. We left so quickly that we didn't take anything with us. I left that six-shooter and bandoleer that I found in there," James lamented.

"It sucks, but we'll find something else," John repeated.

"There's no use trying to hold on to anything in this world anymore," Bob chimed in. "I was hoping that I'd be an old man before I realized that everything is temporary."

"Let's just focus on getting a car. I don't like being out here like this," Lucas said.

"I'm scared," Diego whined quietly.

"Don't be scared. We're okay. Trust me," Sandrine said to him and grabbed his hand. "You're a Side Hooligan now."

"I'm a what?"

"Side Hooligan," she said slowly. "It's our club. You're in it now."

They walked for forty-five minutes before they found a car they could get running. James hot-wired it and then dodged questions about how he knew how to do that. He told them it was something that they all needed to know now. He would teach them. His hair hung in his eyes in sweaty tendrils. He was going to arrange a hair cutting party when they got back to the house since everyone's hair was looking long and shaggy.

They had found a 1993 Jeep Grand Cherokee. Already a gas hog, there wasn't much gas in the tank. James hit the pedal and said a silent prayer that they would make it back to the house before the tank ran dry. He wanted to push it and try to get back to their house as quickly as possible since the roads weren't something that could be trusted anymore. If he was careful and didn't encounter any obstacles, they could be back home within an hour.

Lucas sat beside him in the other front bucket seat with the window down and his arm resting on the sill working on his farmer's tan. The remaining four were jammed into the backseat. Bob and John were like bookends against the doors with the two young kids between them. Bob and Diego bickered about Diego keeping his seatbelt on. Diego was terrified that he wouldn't be able to get out quick if needed to. Bob was terrified that Diego would go through the windshield if something happened.

Once the seatbelt matter was settled, they rode along chattering to one another. Sandrine was excited to get back and see how their garden was doing. In the almost two weeks that they were gone, she bet that they would have a lot of vegetables and berries to eat.

Up ahead about an eighth of a mile, a truck pulled out of side street and headed toward them. It sped toward them on the narrow road. His arm hung out the rolled down window slapping at the door panel. As he passed the Jeep, he slowed to look at its occupants and they looked back at him.

Lucas sped up. He looked in the rearview to see the truck turning around in the road. Before the truck had completed the turn, Lucas turned down the crossroad that the truck had come from. "Wasn't that our truck?"

"Sure was. Pull in down there!" John said pointing to a barn set back from the road with a house set back even further. "We can pull in behind the barn or house."

Lucas agreed and he sped down the long drive and he pulled the Jeep behind the house. They boys got out and peered around the side of the house, looking down the drive. The dust from the dirt driveway was settling back down in the tracks from the tires. James and Bob ran across the drive to peer out from some blueberry bushes.

The truck pulled down the street and stopped just past the barn. He driver got out and looked around. He didn't notice the last remnants of the dust still floating above the ground down by the house.

"Why did you drive away?" He yelled. "I just wanted to talk to somebody." He stood with his hands on his hips, turning and looking. He wiped his face with one hand. "I just wanted to talk to *somebody*." He got back into the truck and continued down the road.

When he was out of sight, they all got back into the Jeep. The commotion brought out a cannibal animal couple. Maybe they had lived in the house or maybe they had gotten lost in the woods. They all took guesses at who this couple of stiffs could be. Was this the new car game? They went back to the road they had left and continued on their way.

The house looked much the same as it had when they had set out on set on their journey. Lucas had to caution Sandrine about just jumping out of the Jeep and running to look at the garden. Since they'd left Bob and Diego's house, he'd noticed a confidence in her now that there was someone in the group less capable than she was. He didn't want that newfound confidence to put her in danger. The world was a dangerous place in ways they'd never imagined before all this happened.

They stopped at the garden and noticed that it had grown quite a bit in the two weeks during their absence. The previous owners of the house had planted this bounty back before the shit hit the fan. There were vegetables forming buds and they could start to identify what was growing where there hadn't been a stick with a name. Green tomatoes and red and green cherry tomatoes hung on the vines. There were also plenty of weeds. There were so many weeds that occupied their garden that pulling them all would keep them plenty busy for a good week.

Sandrine headed for the door. Lucas stopped her, asked her to wait. It was either her confidence or her mistaken belief that the world was still good that stopped her from considering that the house may no longer be safe. He told her to wait outside with Diego until someone said it was okay to come inside.

Lucas turned the doorknob and slowly entered with his handgun drawn and ready to fire. The entrance opened into a large kitchen. Countertops, cabinets and appliances lined the walls. A breakfast table sat in a corner with chairs huddled around it. The kitchen was unchanged from when they left.

James came in behind him and they split off to different parts of the house. Each boy carefully checked closets, corners, under beds and behind furniture and nothing seemed amiss. John came in last and scanned through the basement. The three met each other back in the kitchen and told the others it was okay to come in.

One by one they came through the kitchen and headed to their rooms. Sandrine went straight to the room that she shared with Lucas. She looked at her bed and frowned. It wasn't right, she thought. Where's Margot? I made my bed before I left and it's messy, she said to herself. She pulled back the blankets, looked under the bed, opened the closet and there was no Margot.

"What up, hooligan?" Lucas asked, dropping his backpack on his bed.

"I can't find Margot."

"You didn't take her on our adventure?"

"I didn't want to lose her or for her to get dirty so, I left her here. I made my bed and I left her here. Now my bed is a mess and she's gone," the girl complained.

They discussed it a little further and then the subject was dropped. Lucas assured her that Margot would turn up and then teased her about making her bed when it wasn't something she typically did. They'd had a long day, he said. She'd find the doll tomorrow.

The hooligans gathered in the kitchen. There was a bowl of green tomatoes and several too small cucumbers on the table along with a few opened cans with spoons poking out of them.

"Looks like dinner is served," John commented.

"Nothing but the best for a fine diner like you," Bob quipped as he grabbed some cutlery from a drawer and then opened the cabinet door to get some plates. The inside of the cabinet door had a name carved into it. Neither of the boys noticed this. Bob called for the rest telling them that dinner was ready.

He had been out looking in the neighborhood for supplies. It had been a delight to go through his neighbor's homes. The neighbors that had teased him, pointed at him, screamed horrible things at him and neighborhood kids that had beaten him from time to time. He had found all sorts of fun things in the neighbor's houses. Guns, a leather coat, lots of money, and a really cool ring with a diamond in a bevel setting on a dark band. He put the ring on his middle finger immediately. He went to a mirror and started flipping himself off and he liked the way it looked. A lot.

The last house he hit was two doors down from his own. It had been pretty quiet over there for the last week. He hadn't heard the dog at all since he couldn't remember when.

He broke the latch on the screen door of the porch and then when finding that the front door was locked, he broke the long window glass to the side of the door that was closest to the doorknob. He reached in and flipped the deadbolt and the lock on the knob and let himself in. Once inside, he could hear the faint barking of the dog coming from somewhere in the house. He'd check that out later. First, he wanted to see what the Mrs. of the house had hanging in her closet.

He rummaged through her drawers and found a very pretty slip that he tried to wiggle into but couldn't. Hazel had called this woman a 'slip of a gal' many a time. He wasn't exactly sure what that meant. The slip might have fit him a couple weeks ago, but not now. He'd gained some weight recently since Hazel was no longer cooking for him. He knew that she was slowly poisoning him so he ate sparingly when she fed him and then gobbled up anything else that he could get his hands on that she hadn't prepared. He did like her fried chicken, though, poisoned or not.

His shoulders and chest seemed to have filled out a bit. His waist was still slim, but he was getting a little bit of a belly. He liked to cup it in his hand like he was holding something. This was something new to him. All his pants had elastic waist bands which weren't getting tighter, but the legs of the pants were getting snugger. He fancied himself building muscles with all his recent activity.

He'd finally freed the small mutt from the basement. It was scratching at the door yelping to be let out. When he opened the door, the dog raced into the house running from room to room and not finding his master at home. He went down in the basement to look for more treasure and only found a dirt floor, stone foundation and a slovenly kept laundry room.

He put the dog on its leash and walked the dog back over to his house. The dog seemed happy to have someone to follow. Hazel was really going to be excited to have a dog at last. Now that the neighbors had all left there was no one to complain.

They'd had a dog once. They'd both loved having the dog, but the neighbors complained to the police about them abusing the dog. Sometimes, he would throw rocks at the dog for target practice. He would catch rats and other small animals in the yard and woods behind the house. He'd cut them up and feed them to the dog. Other times, he'd hit the dog for not doing what he wanted. With all that, the neighbors complained that he and Hazel never brought the dog inside when the weather was extreme. Stupid neighbors! Didn't they know that dogs were bred to live outside? Dogs were animals, after all.

Now, they had a second chance. They could have a dog with no one to complain. Hazel would love the company.

He brought the dog to the backyard, where Hazel was. He connected the dog's leash to the second hook on the run that Hazel was on. He had to be quick and careful. Hazel had spotted him the second he stepped into the backyard and she was already making her way over to him. She walked much better now. She was still slow, but she didn't need her walker anymore.

"Look it, Hazel! Look what I brought us. We have a dog again. The neighbors just left him, so I took him. You will have company. Maybe that will make you happy," he told her.

He stood back out of reach and watched with glee. The little dog stood its ground barking and growling as Hazel approached with her arms stretched out wanting to take the little dog in her arms. When the dog thought that Hazel was getting too close it would move further out.

At one point, the dog stood on its back paws stretching to get away from her before it realized that it could run in the opposite direction which it did. The dog's line tripped Hazel as it ran away. Then, it could only go so far because its line hook could only pull Hazel's along until the line became taut and could go no further until Hazel was moving again.

The little dog ran in circles trying to get free with no luck. The Boy watched the antics of the dog and laughed so hard that he was crying. This was great fun. Finally, he could have some fun. Even Hazel was finally having some fun.

Hazel regained her feet and was slowly making her way toward the dog. The dog barked deep guttural barks and with growls coming from deep within it. Its hair was straight up on its back. When it barked, it bounced a bit off the ground. It would move like a boxer with fancy foot work trying to stay as far away from Hazel as it could.

The dog ran around Hazel and tripping her again. This time, the dog's run was tangled around Hazel's legs and Hazel's run. As Hazel turned her body, it dragged the dog closer to her. The dog pushed its body back on its hind legs trying to keep distance between it and her. The boy clapped his hands in excitement and joy. This was a great show. The best one yet!

Hazel tangled her own arm in the runs, forcing the dog to be pulled ever closer. The Boy stopped breathing. He was excited to see what came next. Would the dog be able to pull away at the last minute? Would Hazel love the dog to death?

The latter happened. Hazel managed to get her arms wrapped around the dog. The dog pulled and jumped but couldn't get away. The lines were too tangled around the both of them. The dog yelped. Hazel smiled and buried her face deep into the dog's neck. The dog screamed and cried. Hazel kept on. Blood spurted and ran. The Boy clapped and laughed and howled. This was great fun. He'd dreamt of such fun and waited years for this. He had always known that one day he would work things out with Hazel, and he was overjoyed that he finally had.

Once he decided that there was no more to see, he went back into the house. It had been a long afternoon and he wanted to relive every minute of the last bit in his mind. That was ecstatically glorious, and he wanted to run his mind over it again and again. Plus, he wanted to get things ready for his trip back to the house. He prayed in his little mind that she was back, that they had brought the little girl back. He was going to return her doll to her. That would make her happy, he mused. Thoughts of seeing her, talking to her and touching her raced through his mind and then he truly did know ecstasy.

I'm trying to move on. I am, but what happened with the Asshole Troop keeps pulling me back. I see something, I think something, and the memories come over me in waves, and then I'm crippled. In this world, there's no affording that. A good friend gave me some good advice, get it out. Write it out. And then this good friend gave me a diary to do just that. Honestly, I don't know if it will help. I'm hoping it does. I just want to get these memories out of my mind!

When I say that first night was the worst night of my life, I never have to question it no matter what has come or will come. When I talk about the things I've done to survive, I'm talking about this night. The stuff of a woman's nightmares was lived out in full living color, pure terror, torture and pain. After that I was just numb the whole time that I was with them.

I was hiding in the field when I was picked up from the ground by my hair. I couldn't stop screaming, it hurt so bad. Little did I know what pain was. It felt like some of my hair came out at the root, and I discovered later, it had.

I came to know that it was Billy that pulled me out of the field and back to the house by my hair. My hands were up at the roots of my hair trying to keep it in my head and to try to lessen the pain. When he got me back to the house that Kenya and I had just searched for supplies, he threw me on the ground and kicked me in the stomach and I just curled up into a ball. I started crying and my tears fell into the dirt.

He stood over me. He pulled a flask out of his back pocket and took a long swig. He held it out to me asking if I wanted a swig from a flask that said on it, "Fuck my liver." I'd never seen anything like that before. I said I didn't. I didn't want to drink from something he'd had his mouth all over. He told me to never mind.

I'd want it later and he wouldn't give me any then. What I wanted later was a bullet and a gun.

I was left crumpled in a ball at the feet of the woman that I had seen earlier. If she had bent to comfort me, talk to me or help me, I wasn't sure. I was too wrapped up in the pain and fear that I was feeling. I was glad that I had sent Kenya to my girls.

Billy started hitting the woman for trying to console me. She cowered near me. At one point she was leaning against me. She had her hands up protect her head from the blows he was giving her.

There was laughter and cat calls as the other men came around to take a look at me. They had been hoping for someone much younger, hotter. One of them said that one bitch was as good as another.

We stayed at that house that night. The sun had set not too long after they grabbed me. They pulled out what food they had and lazily ate sitting around in the living room of the house. They offered me nothing. The woman ate from cans that had been discarded by the men. Billy drank like his flask was bottomless.

Later, they made me take my clothes off and then they just assaulted me. I'm not going to go into detail. I can't. I don't want to see it in my mind's eye as one continuous reel. I remember Billy standing over me and pulling out his flask. He poured the whiskey onto my cut and torn body, and it stung like hell. "Let's drink, bitch!" He said. He did this every single time. It's bad enough that images of my time with them pop up out of nowhere from time to time, but I can still hear his deep and gruff voice, "Let's drink, bitch!"

The woman did not survive the night. She died while being tormented by Billy. I was having my own tormenting at the time. Billy defecated on her and put her outside. He didn't neutralize her; he just put her outside. I never even knew her name. Her body wasn't there the next morning. She must have wandered off. I never saw her again.

My time with the Asshole Troop was beyond hell, any imagining of hell, Stephen King can't even touch it. I was pummeled and prodded endlessly and that was putting it politely. It only stopped when they all slept. My only solace, the only way I got through this was knowing that my girls were with Kenya. I prayed that they were waiting for me at my parent's house. No matter how much I checked out during the debasement of my body, I held onto that hope, and I looked for a way out.

Most days I could barely walk. Every cell in my body screamed out in constant, never ending pain. I was covered in so many bruises that my skin was a palette of colors. I was always hungry and always thirsty. Unless Goner gave me something to eat or drink, I had to sneak it or find something on my own and eat it before they caught me with it.

I hadn't bathed since the last day I left my parent's house. My hair was snarled and matted with blood. I did my best to never catch my reflection. I didn't want to know what I looked like. When I finally did see myself, I cried for hours. I knew it was bad but seeing how bad broke my heart.

When I woke in the morning, before anyone else was up, I would think of my girls. I would pray that they were waiting for me at my parent's house. I knew that as long as Kenya was with them that they would be safe. I was grateful that they only got me and that she was able to get to the kids. Knowing where they were and that they were together kept me going in the roughest moments.

The lowest moments were when I'd think of Kevin and Mike. I would tell them both how much I loved them. I tried to picture their faces, but I couldn't. I could hear Kevin's voice, but I couldn't see him or Mike even if I tried to think of specific instances or memories. They were just blanks.

After being beaten awake one morning for not having a breakfast waiting for the Asshole Troop, I was careful to make sure that I did. Some days, it wasn't easy. We didn't have anything.

It pissed off Billy and Hank that day after day, I was still there. The days melted together, and I survived them by sheer will alone. My surviving challenged them and made it worse for me, more painful for me. I refused to give up and just die no matter how much I wanted to sometimes. One thing I've never understood was why they never just shot me. They shot so many others, but never me. I just didn't make sense.

Was God getting me though this so that I could get back to my girls? Was God controlling the most that he could to keep me alive? I can't imagine that he would let all that happen to me if he could have done more. It must have been the most he could do. All he could accomplish was to keep me alive and broken. In the end, it was enough.

Billy and Hank were the worst of the Asshole Troop. If Billy was the leader, then Hank was his silent partner. Hank was the only one that Billy treated with any level of respect, as if they were equals. The rest of the barbaricfuckpigs deferred to them.

Billy and Hank had owned a general carpentry company together and had been hunting partners before all this went down. They were soaking up this new world and squeezing every drop out of it that they could. They were predators to anything and everything and they reveled in it. It was as if they had been caged their entire lives and had finally been set free to do what they pleased, whatever it was that they wanted to do. They were no longer bound by a moral or legal code. Anything and anyone were fair game.

They captured a teen-aged girl one afternoon. They offered to help her and then, well, you know what happened. I put myself between them and the girl repeatedly. I got the beating of a lifetime and then they raped me. I didn't have to be conscious for them. I was just a body. The girl was raped and then killed, and it was worse than usual because I tried to help her. Lesson learned. I think they thought my beating would do me in, but it didn't. I just kept cycling through the faces of my five girls.

We drove from place to place, always scavenging. The longest we stayed in one place was for three nights and that was only because they were trying to fix something on the truck and look for a backup vehicle. Usually, it was one night and then we moved on. Life was nomadic and temporary; temporary, quite literally, for pretty much anyone that crossed paths with them.

Billy and Hank were somewhere between their late 30's to early 40's. There wasn't small talk between us so I couldn't really say. There was a shorthand between them. The most they spoke was when they were on the hunt or torturing someone. Then they spoke for the fun of taunting their victims.

There was Ralph who talked a blue streak and mostly to himself. He seldom said anything of importance. It was more like a nervous tick than anything else.

He was about twenty-five with greasy, dark hair and surprisingly pale skin for someone that had worked outside his adult life. He had this wooden trunk that he kept. He filled it with the pilfered jewelry he had accumulated. When he lifted the lid, it looked like a pirate's treasure chest filled with sparkling diamonds, gold and precious stones. It must have been him fulfilling some childhood dream or something because none of this stuff held any value any longer.

Gary, Gopher and Goner were related. They all had small foreheads, unibrows and low hairlines. Gary was the older cousin, about twenty or twenty-one. Gopher and Goner were brothers, nineteen and sixteen, respectively. This, I only knew because Gopher and Goner would argue about who was the boss of whom referencing age as the ruling factor. Goner rode roughshod over Gopher constantly.

When it was Gary's "turn", it was get on and get off. Sometimes, he didn't even take his turn. Even when he hit or kicked me it was all a part of his perfunctory performance. If he was the middle of the spectrum, his cousins were at opposite ends. I don't know why they went by Gopher and Goner but, to me, what difference did it make?

Despite being the youngest of the Asshole Troop, Goner was as mean, spiteful and sadistic as Billy and Hank. It was like he was making up for some shortcoming that he didn't want anyone to notice. At times, I felt like an experiment in a serial killer's lab. There was something missing in him. He was slow and meticulous. He looked for my responses and he was in his element when I screamed. God help me, I tried not to since it only made it worse and last longer. I thought he broke my arm one night. Turned out that it was a bad sprain. I'm still surprised that, one, I walked away from them and, two, without any broken bones. One woman was crippled by one of their beatings. When they were done with her, the left her for dead and for the dead heads. Wasn't like she was going to run away. She couldn't move her legs and with a broken arm, she wasn't going to get far.

Gopher was better to me than the rest of them. It was as if he was Goner's alter ego. In the pecking order of things, I think Gopher was just one rung above me. He was often egged on by the others, always pushed to do more than he wanted because they knew that he wanted no part of any of this.

He suffered from such a lack of confidence and low self-esteem that it was exploited to sickening degrees. When no one was looking, he would sneak me food and try to comfort me and I let him. His touch made my skin crawl. His attempts at comfort I could do without, but any special favors like food or water I would take because I needed to survive.

We'd break camp sometime in the mid-morning and pick a direction and go. There was no rush to get anywhere. There was no particular destination in mind most days.

If they saw a group of dead heads, they would pull over and take them all down and enjoy themselves doing it. It reminded me of the old west stories where the cowboys going west on trains shot at buffalo for fun eventually bringing them nearly to extinction. I wonder how their numbers are now.

If we came upon other people, women and children were taken with us, used up and disposed of. The men and babies were eliminated immediately. They were dangerous. I wish I could wipe my brain clean from what I've seen them do.

Sometimes, they would hunt people. It sickened me how much they loved doing that. They would see tracks or evidence of life, set traps, lie in wait and then ambush the target. They'd draw it out like it was great sport and then revel in the kill. If cell phones and social media still worked, they would have posted their trophies online for bragging rights.

It ripped at my soul like pulling string cheese apart one thread at a time. I could do nothing to warn or help these people. If I did, I would most certainly lose my life and never see my girls again and then these people would die anyway. I told myself that getting back to my girls was the purpose those lost lives served. That might sound cold and unfeeling, but I assure you that it was quite the opposite. I was in constant mourning. I had to hold on to the hope that my girls were alive and that I would see them again.

I can't go into any detail about what happened when there were new captives. I can't unsee what I've seen as much as I've prayed for it. I don't think describing their plight would help me any to relive it and would only demean them even further. They dropped like flies because that's what they were to the Asshole Troop; they were no longer human. They had no value just like ants to little boys with magnifying glasses on a sunny day.

What I've seen, I see again every time I breathe. The fear, grief and terror weigh on me like a tattoo, indelible to my skin, a permanent mark to never forget.

Acknowledgements

You can write alone but you can't do it by yourself. The following have been indispensable in the writing and compilation of the collection of the first five issues.

- ♥ Joe Keen
- ♥ Amanda Wood
- ♥ Lisa Zeirenberg
- ♥ Becky Jones
- ♥ Jeff Kingsbury
- ♥ Carolyn Dowers
- ♥ Jordie Witt
- ♥ Cynthia Woods
- ♥ Anne Kerrigan
- ♥ Michelle Bohlen
- ♥ Martha McCall
- ♥ Stephen King
- ♥ Jennifer Smith…for something

Notes

Written in the following locations and circumstances

- △ Atlanta, Georgia while working on Stranger Things, Georgia's DMV, The Gifted, MacGyver, The Doom Patrol, Amazing Stories, Dolly Parton's Heartstrings, The Walking Dead, Black Lightning, Ozark, Sistas, The Oval, Brockmire, Charming the Hearts of Men, Sweet Magnolia, The Reckoning, The Resident, Jumangi 2
- △ Nashville while working on Real Country
- △ Vermont while working on The Witch in the Window
- △ Ruskin, Florida while taking some time off
- △ Peachtree City, Georgia while working on Tag
- △ New York, New York while working on The Cromarties
- △ Boston, Massachusetts while working Daddy's Home 2
- △ Miami, Florida while working on I am Frankie

And on that note, if you'd like to write me and ask about certain characters or why I made certain choices, what you liked or hated, or ask how I could miss such a glaring typo please email me at lizzierussell29@gmail.com. I'd love to hear from you and maybe you'll see your email responded to here.

Don't worry pumpkin. There's more.

There's always more...

Made in the USA
Columbia, SC
17 July 2023

20212670R10140